Oren Bell

Oren Bell

BY

Barbara Hood Burgess

Delacorte Press

Published by
Delacorte Press
Bantam Doubleday Dell Publishing Group, Inc.
666 Fifth Avenue
New York, New York 10103

Library of Congress Cataloging in Publication Data

Burgess, Barbara Hood.
    Oren Bell: a novel / by Barbara Hood Burgess.
       p.   cm.
    Summary: Twelve-year-old Oren and his twin sister Latonya come to
terms with the condemned house next door which they believe is haunted
and responsible for many of the tragedies in their lives.
    ISBN 0-385-30325-4
    [1. Dwellings—Fiction.   2. Twins—Fiction.   3. Brothers and sisters—
Fiction.   4. Detroit (Mich.)—Fiction.   5. Afro-Americans—
Fiction.]   I. Title.
PZ7.B916480r   1991
[Fic]—dc20   90-41810
                                                                          CIP
                                                                           AC

Manufactured in the United States of America

Designed by Joseph Rutt

May 1991

10 9 8 7 6 5 4 3 2 1

BVG

To my husband, John, and
to my children: Lee, Chris, Deborah, and Eric

Whenever evil dishonors a place
there are powers to save.

Latonya Bell
Detroit, Michigan, 1982

Chapter 1

○ ○ ○

L atonya flattened him up against the brick wall of the front porch like he was some kind of bug, then she breathed her fresh toothpaste breath all over his face. Oren knew for an absolute truth that he was an hour older than his twin sister; but Latonya was bigger, stronger, smarter, louder, and more trustworthy than him. She looked more like a full-grown woman than his mama did. On days when she needed to go to work early, his mama made Latonya king of the house.

"This is the first day of the new school year and we need to look good. It's final inspection time," the king declared.

His little sister Brenda bounced up and down, happy in her new tennies. Brenda's little braids stood up at attention all over her head. Her twig of a body was tied into new

1

jeans that Latonya expected her to fit into, that is if Brenda ever grew hips. Brenda's yellow shirt had GO TIGERS printed on the front in big black letters. Brenda looked good. Brenda was ready.

"Latonya," Oren pleaded, "both you and me are wearing new shirts with ducks on the pockets." He hated being dressed like Latonya. He hated the first day of school. He hated shirts with ducks on the pockets. "I got on the new underwear," he submitted hopefully.

"Not good enough, Oren Bell," Latonya said. "I'm not all that proud showing up for the important first day of school dressed the same as a low achiever like yourself, but you don't hear me carrying on over it. Our mama worked long, hard hours to buy us these look-alike shirts. Stand tall in your duckie shirt. Who cares what your trash friends say?"

"Latonya," Brenda whined, "when we going to start on the 'reverse-curse ceremony'? When? It's time. It's time. The house next door is waiting and grinning."

"Oh, no," Oren wailed, loud enough that Latonya would know this year he meant business. "I'm not taking part in your voodoo ceremony again this year. Over the summer time, while your chest was filling out, girl, my brain was maturing. You've gone and made your reverse-curse ceremony more important than real ceremonies like blessing the food we eat and pledging to the flag. Brenda is getting weirder by the day, from your example. I'm taking myself back inside our house to wake up Granddaddy. Granddaddy says if there be any ghosts or ill winds coming out of the house next door, your ceremony only serves to rile 'em up. Granddaddy says your ceremony is a crock full of superstitious nincompoopery. Granddaddy says a house don't have the sense to know when it's being reverse cursed. Granddaddy says I don't have to have nothing to do with your baby games."

"We start up the ceremony as soon as our cousins, Dink and Dede, come downstairs from their upstairs flat, and you are going to start up with us. The ceremony has kept us safe from human violence, unexplained phenomena, and everyday plain bad luck for all of our growing-up years. We aren't going to anger that evil house until we get Brenda safely through S. S. Elementary School. Do you hear me, Oren Dumb Bell?"

The whole city of Detroit could hear Latonya when she talked, but not many bothered to listen. Oren, however, knew that she had the power and the command. Granddaddy was older and had gone to school more years than Latonya, but common sense never came into who got to be boss in the Bell house. Oren heard his cousins stomping down the steps, but he knew he couldn't count on them for support. It wasn't Christian to hate cousins, so he didn't actually waste good hate on them. Cousin Dink was in the same seventh grade as Latonya and Oren. Cousin Dede was around the same eight years old as Brenda. Oren's aunt Grace believed her children were more refined than other kids, but she was their mama and so entitled. Aunt Grace permitted her precious boy and girl to walk to school with Oren and his sisters, only because Latonya provided protection for all who walked near her. Aunt Grace also allowed the cousins to take part in Latonya's reverse-curse ceremony against the house next door. His aunt had written complaining letters about the deserted, boarded-up wreck to the mayor of the city of Detroit, to the *Detroit News,* and to the *Detroit Free Press.* Her letters had brought forth no action, so Latonya's ceremony appeared to be Aunt Grace's best shot against the evil house. Despite the safe conduct to and from school that Latonya provided for Dink and Dede, the cousins were not permitted to associate or otherwise hang around with Oren and his sisters after school hours. Aunt Grace believed that the downstairs Bells were unfit to associate with the upstair Bells. Aunt Grace thought Latonya was too smart, Oren was too dumb, and Brenda was too weird. Aunt Grace aimed straight for medium in raising Dink and Dede.

Sometimes Oren avoided looking at Dink for days, but today he looked and froze. Dink had a duck on the pocket of his new shirt. Oren knew his mama to be a kind lady, but when there was a basement sale at the J. L. Hudson Company, his mama turned mean.

"It's time for the ceremony," Latonya told them, ignoring the duck on Dink's shirt.

"May I explain the rules?" Brenda pleaded. "Pleeeeze let me, Latonya. I did help make them up. I need to make the rules very clear. If Oren screws up like he did last year, then the schoolchildren of Detroit are in for a wrongful year."

"We all know the rules, Brenda. We have to trust that Oren will not screw up again this year and ruin innocent lives."

Latonya marched her little company of Bells down the steps.

The whole thing was foolish to death, but Oren went along. What choice did he have? The five Bells stopped dead at their own lot line, pausing like they were about to make a dangerous crossing. Oren looked back at their own

friendly home and took pleasure from the s
family rented their condemned house from t
troit for ninety-eight dollars a month. There   ⌐ɪean,
bright pride about their old pink brick. The Bell flat had
been condemned for as many years as they had lived in it,
but the Lodge Freeway had passed over it and didn't seem
to need it. Latonya made the windows sparkle. Oren
mowed the grass. The early September sun had warmed
and spread out Brenda's marigolds into a wild explosion of
orange and yellow. Oren shifted his gaze across a weedy lot
to the house next door. It was the only other house standing on the block. Each day of the school year, the cousins
needed to pass this majestic, empty-eyed monster in order
to get to the safety of the corner. Latonya claimed that
longtime neglect made it mean and ugly. Bums and winos
often slept the night in the house, but there never was a
steady, God-fearing person living inside to love and care for
the old ruin. Latonya believed the house was out to get
decent people. She could be right. It was known that dangerous stuff went on inside the house. Once a city inspector
had been found dead in one of its upstairs closets. There
had not been a mark on his poor stricken body.

The house was a sorry sight to behold. Aunt Grace called
it a blight on their neighborhood.

"Don't you dare stick your toe over the line before your
time, Oren," Latonya warned him, "and don't you ever forget what happened because of what you did last year. You,
Oren Bell, opened your eyes before you fully passed by the
house, thereby sticking all of us innocent people with bad
luck. As a result of your blunder, we all paid the price. Last
year, if your mature brain can recall, when we arrived at the

doors of the school, we discovered the teachers were out on strike and they stayed out on strike until Halloween. It was your fault, Oren. You angered the house, and closed down the doors of all the Detroit schools for two months. Don't you ever do that again."

"Have a heart, Latonya. Not everybody in Detroit thought the school closing was hard news."

"Oren, why don't you believe in what's been proven time and time again? You go first, Dink. Say a reverse curse. Walk backward past the house without once opening your eyes. When you are safely past the wicked place, we'll all yell and give you notice."

"I have never opened my eyes too soon and brought down terrible luck on my friends," Dink reminded them proudly.

Oren gave credit where credit was due. Dink had not opened his eyes during the crucial crossing, but Dink delivered the most simpleminded reverse curse in the universe. The house should eat him alive for saying such junk out loud.

"Old house," Dink bawled, "you stink. Rot and fall down. Down fall and rot. Stink you, house old."

Pleased with his effort, Dink positioned himself for his backward walk. Oren sat down on the grass, but kept his eye on the house next door. He knew Dink to be a slow and careful backward walker. He watched to see how the house took to Dink. The house had what looked like a face, with eyes, nose, and a mouth. It was grinning at Dink. Who could blame it? The eyes were two long windows on the third level. Besides being long and narrow, the eye windows were bloodred. Latonya said the top windows were reverse church stained glass and protected by the devil. The fact that the red windows were unbroken and not boarded up suggested that the house might possess some dark and evil force. Oren's friend Fred Lightfoot had been throwing rocks at the red windows since he was a kid, and Fred was a high thrower. Other kids had attempted to put out the red eyes, but no rock had ever hit home. The middle floor had only one boarded-up window because there was a staircase on that side of the house. Fred Lightfoot had been inside the house and told them so. The middle window was round and looked like a runny nose. The main floor had a row of boarded-up windows that looked like grim, dirty teeth. Vandals and even ordinary people had written their names, four-letter swearwords, and love words on the teeth. Dink finally reached the other side safely, and it was time for little Dede to go. Dede was too young to say many words in reverse, although Oren's little sister Brenda was the same age and she could talk in reverse all day, if she felt like it.

Dede said, "Boo to you, house. House you to boo." She took little zigzig steps backward, while Latonya screamed at her to guide the way.

It was Brenda's turn. Brenda gave excellent reverse curses. Brenda was a child genius and weird in more ways than one. His Granddaddy thought so. Brenda could talk up to haunted houses easy. That was because she had a pet ghost who lived under her bed. Oren had never actually seen Brenda's ghost, but Latonya slept in the same bed with their little sister, and she believed Brenda's ghost had some substance. Of course, Granddaddy said there was no such thing as ghosts, but he did admit that every rule had to have

one exception, and he thought Brenda's ghost might well
be the exception to the "no such thing as ghosts" rule.

Brenda sang out in her high, fluty little-girl voice,

Fee Fi Fo Fum
bones and blood
and lots of scum.
Fee Fi Fo Fum
bones and blood
and rums and bums
that's what haunted
houses are made of.

Fum Fo Fi Fee
Blood and bones
Scum of lots and
Fum Fo Fi Fee
Blood and bones
Bums and rums and
Haunted what that's
of made are houses.

"Enough is enough, Brenda," Latonya said. "Oren and
me need a turn. You'd reverse curse all day, if we let you.
Close your eyes and start back stepping."

Brenda's little body shot back, straight as an arrow to the
mark. Brenda had perfect coordination. Her gym teacher at
S. S. Elementary said so.

Now it was Latonya's turn. Latonya intended to give the
same reverse curse as she had the year before. Oren's twin
sister talked in the same pushy way to haunted houses as

she talked to him and everybody else. It was pitiful to listen to her. While Latonya was raving and ranting in reverse at the house, Oren watched to see if the face of it changed expression. The house stayed cool. He thought that he saw a face peering out one of the house's bloody eyes, but it was hard to tell for sure. It might be his friend, Fred Light-foot. Fred was fearless.

"Oren Bell, give a reverse curse and get yourself over here backwards on the double. We are all waiting and pray-ing that you do not screw up again. Do it right, so we can get on with the school year."

He waved to Latonya to shut her face. He hated giving a reverse curse to a thing that was not human. Why should he give evil the comfort of talking to it? His voice was naturally too low for Latonya to hear if he was reverse cursing or not, but no matter how outlandish Latonya got in her dictates, he was afraid to deceive her. He usually ended up by trying to humor her, but her crazy ideas were made up with com-plicated systems that gave him trouble. In his mind he thought up the worst curse word in the world. and then he thought of one that was worse than that one. His mama didn't like him to talk or think dirty, and Latonya said there was an invisible spirit checking on his words and thoughts when she wasn't around to do it. She was probably using Brenda's ghost to snoop inside his head. Any word was allowed for reverse cursing, but he didn't know how to talk or think in reverse. He couldn't even seem to reverse a word with only four letters. Latonya was getting impatient. He gave the house a reverse finger. The house looked back at him. It was mad. Man, was it mad. He turned his back on the house and began his backward hike. Right from the beginning he knew the walk was not going well. His gym teacher had never told him he had coordination. Walking backwards made him seasick. He kept going off into the weeds. He could hear Latonya's hysterical screams, but the sound didn't give him direction. He didn't know north from south, or right from left anymore. There was a sick blob of panic hitting under his heart. He couldn't swallow his own spit. He was sweating. It was a heart attack coming on for sure. If he fell dead at the steps of the house, it would be embarrassing. A girl, two little kids, and one fool had finished the walk before him with no trouble. Here he was, Oren Bell, screwing up the ceremony again. He opened and squinted one eye just a sliver of a slit for just a second to right his progress. He didn't care if the house saw him do it, as long as Latonya didn't see him. Now he knew where he was going. He let himself fall into the weeds enough times so nobody would be the wiser. He took the last steps with his eyes shut tight, stumbling drunkenly over the line to safety. He gave a mock bow to the house, and then turned and bowed to his sisters and cousins.

"Very good, Oren. You made it fair and square and we are proud of you. We doubted you had the skill to succeed, but you came through. Now we will all enjoy safe passage and good luck for the whole school year. We can pass by the house each day unafraid. Feel free to go off and join your trash friends. But mind, you had better show up at school on time or it will break your mother's heart."

His brothers were sitting on the grass by the street sign waiting for him. There was Basil Brown, who was called Blue. There was John Wayne Whitefield, who was called

Whitey. Fred Lightfoot answered to Fred Lightfoot and that's all. Blue and Whitey had families like Oren's. Fred Lightfoot had been born a foster person, and had no mama, sisters, or brothers to tell him what to do. There was a strange look about Fred. He wasn't black like Oren, Blue, Whitey, or most other people. He wasn't white like some people. He wasn't even Mexican. Fred was a peculiar red-brown shade, and he claimed to be a 100 percent American Indian. It couldn't have been Fred's face that Oren had seen in the window. The fact was, it was most likely a bum or a wino or some junkie who had a right to be in the house. Oren saluted his brothers, and they saluted him back. Their salute was a cool and mazy set of dance steps with secret arm movements. They didn't say a word about the ceremony. Oren was prepared to be ribbed, jeered, razzed, and poked over all the way to school. He could wait. They had probably rehearsed something awesome.

They started slowly together, taking the long way to school. There were gangs in the neighborhood, and some might have accepted Oren or Blue and Whitey, but their mamas and Latonya wouldn't let them join such organizations. All the gangs wanted Fred for their membership, but Fred believed gangs were too crowded for independent thinkers. Four was all he allowed in his company. Their private club had no rules and no obligations. They'd been together since the third grade. Whitey was older, but he had flunked a grade a few years earlier to stay by them. It was more cool to belong to Fred's Four than to a gang. Besides, Latonya believed a gang of four was safe. Ha. Oren wondered when his brothers were going to start giving it to him for taking part in Latonya's ceremony.

"Oren, nice shirt you have on," Blue finally said with genuine sincerity. "Like that duck."

Whitey nodded his appreciation for the duckie shirt. He also had on a new shirt. Fred was wearing the same clothes he had worn all summer. They walked two by two together past other boarded-up houses, through fields, winding their way to the expressway. Finally Blue brought it up.

"About the ceremony, Oren."

"Yeah." Oren kicked a beer can to show how much he cared about the ceremony.

"You didn't open your eyes, did you?" Blue looked worried like he was hoping that Oren had kept his eyes shut, but he was not all that sure that he had.

For a moment, Oren considered telling them the truth, then he thought better of it. Blue might tell somebody, who might tell another person, who might tell somebody else, who would for sure tell Latonya. Latonya would never forgive him or ever let him forget. The ceremony didn't mean anything anyway.

"Hell and the devil's red ass, Blue. I kept my eyes closed, but why do you care?"

"There's some layoffs coming up on the Detroit police force. My brother could be one of them, if the house gets down on us."

"Hey," Whitey put in. "You did screw up last year, Oren. I don't want there to be another strike by the Detroit school teachers. This is my second try at the seventh grade. If there's another strike, I'll never make it to high school. I'll be finished."

He had never heard such serious talk coming out of Whitey's mouth before, especially about school. The word *finish* sounded a lot like the word *dead.* "Why will you be finished?" he said.

"I'm talking about life, Oren. I'll never make it in life without an elementary-school education. My mama says so all the time."

"I didn't open my eyes," Oren lied.

Fred pointed his finger at Oren and said, "Man, you had better have kept everything above your nose closed." Fred had actually been inside the house many times, so when he came up with an opinion, they listened. Oren hadn't wanted to be responsible for another teachers' strike, although he had enjoyed the last one. What had he done? Latonya's main ambition was to become a doctor in charge of a whole hospital. Another teachers' strike would set her back.

Yesterday, he and his brothers had spent a day on Belle Isle picking up returnable bottles and cans for the deposit. Good honest work. Fred had rolled a bum and taken a little change, but that was no big sin. They had been brothers. He could tell them confidential stuff that would jolt a priest. Now he feared telling them that he had opened one eye a slit of a squint during a stupid ceremony, one that his crazy sisters had thought up. If a lot of bad luck started happening to people around Detroit, he would take the blame for it. The four of them walked along in stiff silence. Oren could feel them suspecting him.

"Hey, look," he said, trying to lighten the mood a little. He pointed to a burned-out hole that had been a beer and wine store the last time he'd been on Third Street. "What happened to Pinky's Party Store?"

"You blind and deaf, Oren?" Whitey asked. "The sirens kept me awake most of the night."

"Sirens never keep me awake," Oren said.

"Who'd sleep if they did?" Blue agreed. "A night don't go by, but that there's fires around the neighborhood. I hear somebody torched Pinky's place."

A common, everyday, burned-out party store sure wasn't going to put them off the subject. The bridge over the expressway offered Oren another diversion.

"Look at the cop cars at the side of the expressway." He tried to sound like this was some kind of a big deal. "Wonder what's up?"

For a moment, the brothers looked down on the steady stream of cars coming into and going out of the city. They noted the cop car parked under the bridge with moderate interest.

"A stakeout to catch the expressway sniper." Blue, the expert on cop activity, told them what they already knew. "The sniper is due to get his next victim this week."

Ordinary things were not going to do the trick. He could tell that Blue was getting ready to bring it up again. He needed to come up with something big that would fill up their attention.

"You think they're going to let the four of us back inside the school this year? After what we did last year?"

"What did we do?" Fred said, like he didn't care.

"We ran Miss Bobb, our homeroom teacher, right out of the school. Poor old Bobb had to go before her time and give up a fat pension fund."

"Oh, yeah, we did that." Fred shrugged.

"Bobb told the school board that Fred was trying to push her out the third-story window." Blue finally helped Oren out.

"The woman was psycho. I think she's doing time in the psycho ward right now." Fred gave the brothers his wicked Indian wolf wink. He remembered and he was proud.

Oren pressed on while he had their attention. "Drove her straight to the psycho ward. You did a job on Bobb, Fred."

"I think it was the fault of that chicken principal, Mr. Meeker," Blue said. "Where was Weaker Meeker when poor old Bobb needed him?"

"He was hiding in his office, where he always is when there's trouble. Meeker is the one we got to run out this year." Fred was really getting into the subject.

"I was never involved in that action, but I heard about it," Whitey said.

"You did more than hear about it." Oren worked on Whitey. "You were the one who supplied the live snake and the dead loon's head. All we did was put them in her purse."

"Poor woman was going to retire to a motel in Disney World and have a happy old age until you guys got on her," Blue snickered.

If he could keep it going for another half block, the ceremony would be forgotten forever.

"I heard it was a racial issue. Miss Bobb said we hated her because she was white." Oren's thoughtful tone gave the subject a little needed seriousness.

All four hooted over this charge. There were white kids in the class who had enjoyed watching Miss Bobb go crazy. Oren was on a roll. He had plenty of other Bobb episodes to throw on the fire. Until the first bell rang, his friends would be busy recalling the fall of Miss Bobb. Oren felt a little guilty. He had done his part in bringing Bobb down, maybe even got the workings of it going in the first place, but he was actually sorry for what had happened to the poor lady. That was the difference between him and his friends. They were never sorry for trouble they caused, like he most always was. After Bobb went down the tube, there had been ten substitute teachers. Latonya had counted them and she remembered most of them by name. Dink Bell said that he had learned something from each one, but he never said what it was. Meeker had promoted the entire sixth grade because there was no sane person left to sort out the fails from the passes.

The school yard was about cleared. Latonya was waiting for them on the steps.

"You guys get in here. The bells don't work. Our room is on the third floor again. Fred Lightfoot, you'd better not try pushing the new teacher out the window. With Oren successfully getting by the house and completing the ceremony, we should be in for a good year."

"For your sake, Bell, we'd better have a good one." When Fred Lightfoot pointed his finger at a person, that person knew he meant business.

"We're going to have an excellent one," Oren said. "I gave that old devil house a reverse-curse it won't forget in a million years."

They raised their arms in a secret brother salute and danced up the steps.

"Ants in your pants, brains in your feet," Latonya said. She held the door open for them and her smile was hopeful.

Chapter 2

○ ○ ○

For a fifth-grade assignment, Latonya had written a poem that didn't rhyme, describing S. S. Elementary School. Oren's mama had saved Latonya's great masterpiece in the event that the Bell family ever had a visitor who would listen to it. What Latonya had written was:

S. S. Elementary rises like a calm castle above the busy Lodge Freeway.
S.S. looks down on the cars and trucks coming in to Detroit and going out of Detroit.
S.S. was designed and built by a person who lived in days of old and liked children.
S.S. is planted in cement and will live forever.

Latonya's poem about their school was a little better than anything the rest of the class thought up, but it didn't give the big picture. There was an important specialness about S.S. that Latonya had left out of her poem. His mama said that music and art programs were called frills, and had long ago been voted out of other Detroit schools. S.S. students had frills drilled into them from kindergarten through the eighth grade. Kids from other parts of the city were invited to take advantage of the programs, but not many ever did. Latonya was both an actress and a horn player. Brenda's pictures were displayed on the walls of S.S. Oren was a trumpet player like his Granddaddy. There was talk each year over closing S.S., but Oren knew they never would. Latonya was right on that score.

"Wonder who our new teacher will be?" Blue said as they walked four abreast up the wide staircase.

"I bet they went out and hired a big man to take our class." Whitey considered. "A professional wrestler who wrestles bears and tigers when he's not teaching."

"A karate expert. A hulk. An invincible robot," Oren guessed.

"Who cares?" Fred said.

The truth was, Fred didn't care. He had no parents to make him go to school. He ran his own bookie business to keep himself in cash flow. Fred went to school for laughs and to hang out, and because it was the law. Even Latonya had to admire him for showing up more times than was required.

Fred, Whitey, Blue, and Oren Bell were last to enter the classroom. Heads turned. Oren felt proud. The Four Musketeers was a name for them suggested by his Granddaddy.

Latonya called them Fred and the Three Stooges. The new teacher was writing her name on the board. She was a small woman. Her back was straight and proud, not all hunched over, defeated and fearful like poor Miss Bobb's back had been. A neat Afro hairstyle circled her head like a halo. When she turned around she proved to have a beautiful face. For a flash, Oren felt like he wanted to please her. The feeling went away as quick as it had come.

"My name is Ms. Pat Pugh," the new teacher said, for the benefit of those among them who could not read.

From reading her name on the board, Oren figured she was Ms. Pat Pug, but the way she pronounced it was even funnier. In a steady voice she started to give them her opening speech. The class always stayed quiet for opening speeches. What she said was, "Ladies and gentlemen of S. S. Elementary's seventh-grade class, it has been reported to me that there was some trouble here last year. I do not know who caused the trouble and I do not care to know. I do not believe in looking at records. I am not aware of who has a learning or a behavior problem. You are all starting off with a clean slate."

Oren knew that Latonya didn't want to start off with a clean slate. His sister had been working on her school record for her whole school life, and she expected it to follow her proudly into medical school. It was really lazy of Ms. Pugh not to look at records. Was it fair for Dink to have to start working into his medium slot all over again? Oren, Fred, Whitey, Blue, and a stupid girl named Kimberly Banks were well satisfied and secure in their bottom learning space. There was nothing fair about a clean slate.

Blue's hand went up. "Ms. Peeyoo, your new plan's not fair. Stinks."

Blue had summed it up so well that Oren, Whitey, and Fred just nodded their agreement for the benefit of the rest of the class, who were waiting to see how Fred and the Three Stooges took the new teacher's opening speech.

Ms. Pugh looked around for support and found it in Dink Bell, whose hand had been waving in the air all the time that Blue was trying to talk. Dink was rude.

"Most teachers in the past," Dink said in his high preacher voice, "gave cute names to our learning groups. Our class always liked the names. In the third grade, the slow kids who made all the trouble were called Submarines. That's the best name anybody ever called Fred Lightfoot, John Wayne Whitefield, Basil Brown, Oren Bell, and poor Kimberly Banks. That year, the regular kids, like me, were called Land Crawlers. Latonya Bell, who strives to outshine everybody in order to fulfill herself, was the one Starship in our class. Last year, Miss Bobb couldn't think up any cute names, so she called us onesies, twosies and threesies, but we knew our place."

"Year to year, do many cross over the group lines?" Ms. Pugh asked Dink.

There was no need to read records with Dink waving his hand in the front row. So there was some use for informers.

"No," Dink sadly shook his head, "but last year Wesley Wrigley Fry came in by car from the suburbs. She became a onesie with Latonya."

Fred had stuck Dink's head in the toilet for telling less, but now Fred stayed cool and raised up his hand in the proper way.

"How you plannin' to do?" Fred asked with polite interest.

"What?" Ms. Pugh looked confused, like she didn't understand English.

"How you plannin' to run things? What you intend callin' the dumb kids who will mos' likely keep makin' trouble? What you plan on callin' Latonya and Wesley, who will mos' likely keep shinin'? Forget namin' Dink Bell. He goin' to have an accident and fade 'way fast."

Ms. Pugh looked annoyed and said, "Fred, I can tell that you are a smart boy, but you either have the lazy-mouth disease or you are mocking me. If you want to communicate information or ask questions, speak correctly."

Ms. Pugh dismissed Fred like he was of no account. She turned to the rest of the class. "Each of you has a special talent or you wouldn't be a student in this special school. I intend to help each of you to make the most of your talents. We will have no slow learners or behavior problems in this class."

Latonya and Wesley hummed over that. Dink and his average in-betweens hooted, chuckled, giggled, and squeaked. Fred, Blue, Whitey, and Oren cracked up, fell on the floor, and punched on Kimberly Banks.

Ms. Pugh took a little whistle from around her neck, put it in her mouth and blew. Like an out of control train gone off its track, a tall, wild-eyed black man crashed into the room. The class quieted down. The man stared at them. Like he could be a hit man looking for the target. He could be the hulk who wrestled bears and tigers. He opened his mouth and spoke to them in a deep voice.

"I am Carl Shell. I am at present the bandmaster at

Northwestern High School in Detroit, Michigan, where my marching band has earned a city-wide reputation for style and discipline. I have come down to this S. S. school to give instrumental lessons and to teach style and discipline. If any of you people ever again give Ms. Pugh cause to blow her whistle, heads will bust. When Ms. Pugh blows her whistle, I answer the call. Do you hear me?"

The man left like he had come. Nobody was sure he had been there, but they stayed quiet while they thought it over. Music was important at S.S. The music teacher had more importance than Mr. Meeker, the principal. Ms. Pugh continued outlining her grand plan to end behavior problems.

"To help control our conduct and sharpen our academic skills, we will go on the buddy system. This is how it will work. Each of you will be assigned a buddy. You will be responsible for your buddy's academic progress and behavior, and he or she will be responsible for yours. It may take a while to find the right buddy for each student, but since Dink has pointed out some of the problem areas in the class, I hereby name Latonya Bell as Fred Lightfoot's buddy, and Wesley Wrigley Fry as Oren Bell's buddy. We will work out the rest of the buddy system next week."

Oren refused to believe what his ears were hearing. Ms. Pugh must be putting them on. Appointing Wesley Wrigley Fry as a buddy to himself was what his Granddaddy would call "perpetuating a punitive strategy to encourage long-range suffering." Miss Bobb had never been smart enough to think up such a mean scheme. Wesley Wrigley Fry had pale yellow hair, pale blue eyes, pale pink skin, and milky brains. If Wesley wasn't much to look at, she knew how to get along. She didn't advance herself by honest bossing and

22

studying like his sister Latonya. She didn't make herself
important by informing on people, like Dink Bell did. Wesley was crying herself to the top. A less-than-perfect score
on anything made her lips tremble and her eyes water. If
the teacher ragged out the kid sitting next to her, she cried.
Granddaddy wasn't going to like him having a white
crybaby girl for a buddy. His mama would insist he show
Wesley a kindly face and friendly manner, and never bad-
mouth her. Latonya would agree with his mama on this
attitude and be ready to give full reports when he slipped. It
was a no-win situation. What to do? Then it hit him. Fred
had Latonya for a buddy. Fred would never hold still for
that. Fred would know how to finish off this Pugh woman
quicker than he had Miss Bobb. Ms. Pugh would never get
her pension. They would be taking her off to the nuthouse
before the first week of school was over, and Oren Bell was
not going to be sorry for Ms. Pat Peeyoo.

The first day of school was over, and whether or not he
believed in the ceremony, the curse of the house seemed to
be working against him. He waited for his sisters by the
door. It had been a long armpit of a day. Wesley Wrigley
Fry's mother had finally picked her up in a pale station
wagon and taken her back to the pale neighborhood where
she belonged. He didn't feel much like getting together with
Blue, Whitey, and Fred, and he was sure that they didn't
want to get together with him. Ms. Pugh was setting them
up one against the other. The woman worked fast. Fred was
now a math group leader because Ms. Pugh discovered that
he owned his own bookie business, and this gave her the
idea that he had hidden math skills. Blue and Whitey were

staying after school to sign up for a computer class, because Ms. Pugh had made them computer specialists before they had one lesson in computers. Ms. Pugh knew somehow that Oren was a reader. He hadn't actually read anything for her yet, but she had her ways of knowing. He didn't fit in anywhere for sure in her system, and it was a lonesome and downright scary feeling. What he wanted to do was to get home and talk to his Granddaddy. What was keeping Latonya and Brenda?

"You get out of my face, Latonya." Fred slid slow and easy through the door, and then started to take off.

"You get back here and pick up your new trumpet, Fred Lightfoot. I'll track you down and see that you practice it. This is your buddy, Latonya Bell, talking to you. Stop those feet before I pursue."

Fred came back and took the instrument that Latonya offered him, and then he walked away without a backward glance to Oren.

That was another thing. What was his Granddaddy gonna think when he heard that Fred had won the first chair position in trumpet on his very first try? Oren wanted to stay in the last reading group, but he had always had a strong desire to be first in trumpet. His Granddaddy was a musician. Bells had music in their bones, but Mr. Shell had gone and given Fred the best trumpet in the school, because Mr. Shell believed Fred to be the trumpet player with the most potential. Oren was sitting in the last chair, playing the third part, which had no tune to it at all; and he was assigned to play the oldest, most beat-up trumpet that S.S. still kept around. What was worse, he had nearly ended up with a flute. He had to plead with Mr. Shell to let him stay in the trumpet section. Brenda joined them and she looked happy. He hated it when Brenda looked happy.

"Latonya, Oren, the new art teacher says I possess promise to be an artist. When I get home I am going to start drawing and I'll paint and color and draw every minute for the rest of my life."

"That's fine, Brenda," Latonya said.

"Who cares, Brenda," Oren muttered.

When they passed the house next door, Latonya noted his gloom. "Oren, see how gentle toward us the house seems. I do believe you have defeated it. I appreciate what you did for us, because I know how hard it is for you to walk backwards without opening your eyes."

He glanced back over his shoulder at the house. It was not looking gentle at them. Latonya was no judge of house looks. The eyes, fired by the late afternoon sun, stared at him with evil satisfaction. The round nose of the house was leaking an unhealthy snot. The first floor mouth smirked like it knew an unholy secret. The house was zapping him, and it took enjoyment from his pain.

Without being told, he began to pick up the empty beer cans, booze bottles, and papers from the front lawn of his own home. The cans and bottles were the fault of the house next door. Picking up its dirty leavings made him feel better about ruining the year for himself and all of the people in Detroit, although Granddaddy would assure him that the ceremony was total nincompoopery. His mama came out on the porch to call him in. She liked him neating up their front yard.

"Thank you, Oren," she said.

After a long shift of work cleaning out the rest rooms at the J. L. Hudson Company, his mama drooped some. Tiredness made her eyes dreamy and her smile wishful. Mama was a beautiful woman, not solid built like Latonya or stick skinny like Brenda, but soft and fairy princess like herself.

"Latonya is fixing supper, Oren, how about you and me raking through the house? Company is on their way down."

"Aunt Grace and her folks coming down to eat?" Now he'd never get to talk to Granddaddy.

"They're all coming, including Uncle Penn." Mama gave her one and only boy child a wink.

Uncle Penn was absent from Aunt Grace's home so much of the time that the welfare department awarded her good money for not having him around. Mama and Latonya didn't approve of cheating the welfare people, but they tried not to judge those who did.

Oren's first indoor job was picking up Granddaddy's cigarette butts and empty glasses, and also searching under sofas and chairs for odd underwear, socks, and dropped newspapers. Latonya harped at Granddaddy, Brenda smart mouthed him and Mama asked him nicely, but Granddaddy never stopped doing what he wanted to do. Oren followed the sound of snoring down the long hallway. He stood quietly at Granddaddy's open door. The deadly fumes of Red Rose wine hung heavy. Granddaddy's wasted frame was spread-eagled on the bed like someone had dropped him from the ceiling. Oren had arrived too late to talk to his grandfather, Bill Bell. He joined his mama, who was scrubbing the bathroom. She was bent over the bathtub, so he started wiping the wash bowl to keep her company.

"We got this new buddy system in school, Mama."

"I heard. Latonya told me."

"Once today I nearly got rid of Wesley Wrigley Fry. Mr. Shell told her to get out of the band room because she has braces on her teeth, and shouldn't be blowing a wind instrument. Mr. Shell said she would have to go string along on a cello or something in the string room. I was happy for a minute."

"Then what happened?"

"She cried and carried on and said she was my buddy and would never leave me, so Mr. Shell let her stay and be a drummer girl."

"That might work."

"There's only three school trumpets, Mama. Fred gets to blow the best one and play first part. I get to blow the worst one and play the last part."

"I bet I know who blows the part in between on the medium trumpet, Oren."

No need to reply to that one. A big noise in the kitchen interrupted their private talk.

"I hear Brenda sassing Latonya in the kitchen. You let me finish up here, and you go read your little sister a story to quiet her down for the dinner hour."

Brenda could read nearly as well as Oren, but she loved to hear him read to her. He took his little sister off Latonya's back, and settled her down in the purple bedroom that she shared with Latonya. Under the bed was an assortment of 1947 Classics Illustrated comic books that

Oren had discovered in the attic before Aunt Grace moved in. Aunt Grace now owned the only entrance to the attic.

"What classic story do you want to hear?" he asked Brenda.

"I want *Tom Sawyer* for myself, but Mr. Figment demands you read *Treasure Island.* That ghost is so spoiled, he always wants his own way."

Brenda called her ghost Mr. Figment because Mama said that the ghost was a figment of her imagination.

"Some person in this room is spoiled, Brenda, and I don't believe that it's Mr. Figment. I don't believe in your ghost. I never see him under the bed when I pull out the comic books."

"Do you believe the house next door has evil powers, Oren?"

He felt a chill. Did Brenda suspect that he had copped a squint during the ceremony?

"No, I don't believe the house has powers. We'll read *Treasure Island* for Mr. Figment."

Brenda's wispy little body came close to him, and he hugged her and started to read. He had long ago figured out all of the words, the easy ones and the hard ones. His Granddaddy would wake up refreshed at midnight, and then they could have their talk.

Oren slept on the living room sofa because Bill Bell needed a bedroom to himself. Oren carefully fit his body around the dips and springs in the old sofa, searching for the one position and spot that worked best. The downstairs Bell flat was quiet, and then Latonya's voice shrieked from the purple bedroom.

"Brenda, you're eight years old and not in control. The shame of it. It wasn't Mr. Figment who wet our bed."

No more sounds. He heard the clock chime ten, then one chime for the half hour. He must have dozed off because he missed eleven, but when the clock struck twelve his ears picked up the sounds of the front door opening and closing. Granddaddy was going out on the front porch to have a cigarette. Oren unwound himself from the sofa, and on quiet bare feet, he joined Granddaddy.

Together they regarded the golden dome of the Fisher Building. It was a noble building, and thanks to the fallen houses in the neighborhood they enjoyed a grand view.

"Granddaddy, you took such a long nap that you missed the action of the day."

"Fill me in, Oren, but zip it along. I'm too tired to listen to one of your long, boring stories."

Oren shortened the story of his awful day the best he knew how, and then waited with hope.

"So the new Ms. Pugh gave you a girl for a buddy and a white one at that."

Bill Bell blew smoke from his wheezy lungs while he mused over Oren's misery. "No big deal. I had buddies when I was in the army. They weren't all brothers. I got in fights with some, but mostly I got along the best I could. School buddies are like army buddies. They have to be in the same place as you, doing the same thing, at the same time. It won't kill you to put up with Wesley."

"I bet none of your army buddies cried," Oren injected.

"Some cried. Give the crybaby a break. Let her be your buddy for a while. The companionship of a steady man just might bring the girl around."

Oren moved right along to his next problem. "About Fred getting first chair on the first tryout. Do you think that's fair? I wanted to be first chair. You were always first chair, weren't you?"

Granddaddy didn't take much time on that one. "When you think you can blow the top horn down, you challenge him. That's the way the band system works. Go ahead. Challenge Fred any time you think you can beat him to the blow."

"You think I can blow Fred down next tryout?"

"No, I don't. Fred is a lot like me. He'll hold on to first chair. I hear him jazz on his song flute. He ain't no common ear musician either. The little bugger plays his notes right on, and that's a gift, because he has trouble with words in a book. Fred's a natural trumpet player who can read notes. Not many of his kind around. The kid will be slurring and double-tonguing before the rest of you little dabblers get by your first lesson. What material is the S.S. band working on?"

"The first lesson in our band book is called 'Variations of Twinkle.' Granddaddy, Fred is one hundred percent American Indian. Why should he be more musical than me?" Oren wasn't hearing what he wanted to hear from his grandfather and he was losing heart.

"Oh, dog, Oren. Nobody is ever one hundred percent. Fred brags over his roots, but he don't know where he come from or where he's going any more than the rest of us do. I give him twenty-five percent Indian blood at best. I met a few like him when I was doing small clubs in Louisiana. A little shot of Indian blood appears to give the buggers jive power, but hey, I hate to take away your hope. If you believe in that old turtle racing the bunny story, you can out-practice Fred on the horn. Fred is into bad habits, and he's not one to improve on what the good Lord gave him."

"But Granddaddy, Fred now has Latonya for a buddy."

"Then I think it was smart of you to take the last chair. I've seen good musicians make it, and I've seen bad musicians make it, but I've never seen a medium musician make it."

Oren related his last concern like it wasn't his biggest. "What about the house and the curse, Granddaddy? You don't think me opening my eyes during the ceremony is going to wipe out anybody or give anybody bad luck?"

"The house is dangerous and foul from top to bottom, Oren, but I don't think the old wreck was fully aware that you winked at it."

"It's all nincompoopery, isn't it, Granddaddy?"

"Total nincompoopery, but my advice to you, keep up the lie that you didn't cop a look. If a few sad sacks get down on their luck during the upcoming year, they'll look for somebody to blame. Bell men should avoid taking the blame for anything. Even total nincompoopery."

"Granddaddy, see how its red eyes sort of light up at night. You think there's a candle or flashlight glowing somewhere inside?"

"Can't say. Don't care. I'm going back to bed. You come along too."

After Granddaddy was back in bed, Oren double-checked the lock on the front door. He eased himself onto the sofa. Better not curl around the springs and get comfortable till he had said his prayers. God liked praying people to pray on their backs, so they could look up while they were doing it. A spring pinned him in the middle of his back, but he stayed firm. Praying was taken more serious if a person suffered while doing it. Latonya had pointed out the rules, and she was an expert on praying.

Dear Lord,
Granddaddy did his best to assure me that the ceremony was total nincompoopery, but if you would send our family and friends some good luck, I would consider it a sign that the house has got no hold on us. Thank you. Amen. Your friend, Oren Bell.

Chapter 3

o   o   o

The first few weeks of school, Latonya viewed small thoughts and happenings as uncommon good luck for the family, or as a special opportunity directed to her alone. Oren took an evil omen out of each ordinary incident and experience, but he didn't give in to the feeling. He stepped on cracks in the sidewalk. He let black cats walk in front of him. If he saw a ladder, he'd walk under it. Over and over, he proved to himself that he was not a superstitious person. But what if the house next door was an exception to the superstition rule? Then as an unsuperstitious person he would have no protection against it.

Mr. Shell assigned to Latonya a new musical horn so big that it had no real name, other than "the biggest horn."

Granddaddy said its name was Tuba. Ms. Pugh said it was the school's one and only brass bass. Mr. Shell called it Sousa, but he was quite a kidder. Latonya couldn't carry the misshapen thing by herself, and yet she still insisted on bringing it home from school each afternoon. Worse than that, she practiced it till bedtime, then started up again first thing in the morning. The sound of the horn wasn't loud, but Granddaddy said it provoked his central nerves. On this morning the steady, low belch of the brass monster woke Bill Bell up before his usual time.

"Latonya," Granddaddy moaned, "if you were a lady, you would excuse yourself when you made a noise like that, and then you would have the decency to quit making it. If a moose gets loose in this neighborhood, the animal will find you and make advances."

Latonya took the mouthpiece out of her mouth so she could answer back.

"Granddaddy, Brenda is sick and you have the serious responsibility of caring for her and tending to her while Oren and me are in school. Today, please do not sot yourself with Red Rose wine."

"I cancelled all my appointments to do my duty by Miss Brenda." Granddaddy gave Latonya his usual avoidance of the real issue.

"Granddaddy and me are going to draw all day," Brenda told them. She was happy to be sick but not too sick. "We got rolls of paper that Uncle Penn stole for us from the board of education, and Mama bought us a new box of Crayolas. Oren, you know what our theme to draw on is?"

"No, what?" He didn't know what a theme was, but why let on?

"All of our pictures will be of sad, sunken, or sinking ships," Brenda told him in her prim teacher voice. "Sad, sunken, or sinking ships is what we plan to specialize in."

"Oh," Oren said. Nothing that Brenda ever specialized in surprised him.

"Don't you humor her, Oren." Latonya fussed. "You are the one who is responsible for Brenda's weirdness."

"Am not. You are."

"Not me. You."

"Hey, you twinnies, get that big fluggle tuba tooter out of the living room, so Brenda and me can get to work on our sunken or sinking ships," Granddaddy said.

"Leave Mr. Figment under the bed." Latonya gave Brenda and Granddaddy her parting shot against weirdness, but Oren knew they would ignore Latonya's advice. Before the day was gone, Mr. Figment would come out from under the bed, and Granddaddy would discover a bottle of Red Rose wine hid under his bed.

Oren and Latonya lugged the brass monster past the house next door, with Dink and Dede jogging behind. Latonya felt so secure in the success of her dumb ceremony that she had to run on about it.

"I am having a wonderful year in school. I love Ms. Pugh's interesting projects. I love my Sousa. I think Mr. Shell loves Ms. Pugh, and that's so lovely."

Oren hated Ms. Pugh's screwy projects. He wasn't having a wonderful year in school. Ms. Pugh had set him up to be in the top reading group, which meant that he'd be sitting between Latonya and Wesley Wrigley Fry for the entire school year, which might as well be for life. The house was letting Latonya off the hook and sticking it to him. He supposed that was fair.

Before they had safely cleared by the house, Fred joined them.

"Where'd you come from, Fred Lightfoot?" Latonya barked at her buddy.

His sister was doing a real job on Fred, but sometimes he showed the old brother spirit.

"You want me to tell you where I come from?"

"None of your dirty mouth, Fred. Just now, you came out o' the weeds by the house. Don't deny."

"Who's denying? I stayed the night in the house. My foster mama locked me out, so I went to the house and it took me in. The house is my crib. Whatta you think of that, Latonya?"

"Oh, Fred," Latonya said, "we would have taken you in. I'm your buddy. Why didn't you come to me?"

Fred shrugged and turned his attention to Dink.

"Dink Bell, you help Latonya carry the biggest horn. I got things to talk over with Oren Bell."

"I got my own horn to carry," Dink said.

"Fine and on the line with me, Dinko stinko. Now I got reason to grab you by your ugly ears, haul you inside the house, and leave you there to squeal yourself to death like the chicken pig you is."

Latonya turned. "I won't permit Fred to do any of those things to you, Dink, but there are times when men need time to talk private; so you relieve Oren of Sousa. Be careful. That wonderful instrument cost a thousand dollars."

Dede took the trumpet from her brother, and Latonya and Dink moved the big horn off in the direction of the school. Oren had to admire the way Latonya was becoming quieter and more reasonable. It appeared the buddy system worked both ways. Oren was impressed that Fred still wanted to talk to him. Under Ms. Pugh's screwy new rules, Fred was class big shot. Ms. Pugh said she admired Indians because they were more minority than most minorities. Fred was now top dog in math and music, and with Latonya coaching him in reading, he was ready to move up there too.

"How does it look inside the house?" Oren asked. He'd been meaning to go inside some day himself.

"It still has furniture," Fred said, "and it is bigger and more fancy than your house, but it is full of dirt and holes and spider webs. A clean freak like Latonya would hate it. There are three bathrooms, but none of them flush. The thing that is most terrible about the house is this: upstairs and downstairs, it has a strong ghost smell."

"How does a ghost smell?" Oren pressed.

"Like rotten skin, mummified puke, vampire blood, and rat turds. The house has an old smell that won't quit. I slept the night on a leather sofa bed. I tried turning my nose from the wall to get away from the smell, but it was all around in the air. I think that it's inside my head and lungs and bones, and will be till I die."

"Wow," Oren said. Indians were as brave as they were musical.

"But I don't go inside the place for ghost sniffing, ya know."

"What for, then?"

"Oren, as you know, I've been taking bets from kids and making cash flow from it."

"Sure, you've been doing that since the third grade. Latonya doesn't think it's right, but I don't mind it."

"Well, now I'm onto something bigger. You're my best brother. I could bring you in. First, you have to promise to never tell. Especially Latonya. Honest Injun. Then you have to get over your fear of the house. The house is my place for contact."

"I promise, Honest Injun, not to tell, but Fred, is what you're talking about legal?"

"It's not absolutely unlegal. It's not possible to make big money being all legal."

"You're not going to sell dope to little schoolchildren?" Oren voiced his biggest fear. Then he added his second biggest fear. "You're not taking it yourself, are you?"

"Don't worry. I don't sell the stuff and I don't take the stuff. What I do is run messages and deliver packages and envelopes. When I make my deliveries, I go inside respectable buildings and deliver to neat old guys dressed up in business suits. I stay away from bad habits myself, even if they are respectable. Ms. Pugh told me that bad habits were what defeated the Indian nations. If Chief Pontiac hadn't been a drinker, the whole of Detroit would be Ottawa today. You heard Ms. Pugh tell the story about how the great Indian chief nearly took Detroit and Michigan away from the white people. I want to shun Pontiac's mistakes but still be successful and rich. I'm saving to buy a Porsche by the time I'm sixteen, and I can't do it on a paper route. There is nothing wrong with me making money on other people's bad habits."

"The house next door isn't a crack house, is it?" Oren interrupted.

"My bosses are what you call diversified, Oren. That means they move all kinds of stuff, but strictly on the business end. We call the action I'm involved in a steamer operation. It goes something like this. I contact people who want their cars stolen by expert specialists in the field. Maybe their car has high mileage or needs body work. Why should our client go on making payments on a piece of trash when the insurance company will pay him the full blue-book value? Our organization has highly skilled mechanics in suburban garages who take apart the cars and sell off the parts at a fair price. The whole operation don't rob a soul but the insurance companies, and everybody knows that insurance companies aren't real people. Don't tell Latonya a word of what I just said. Any kind of sin drives her wild, even when only respectable people do it. Do you want in, or not?"

"Not."

"Why?"

"You can call it steaming if you want, but it's still stealing. You're just stealing from more people."

"Give me a break, Oren. Stealing isn't all bad. Ms. Pugh admits that Robin Hood did it when it helped the poor, and I'm poor."

Oren appreciated that Fred had no mama to teach him the evils of stealing; so he decided to try another angle.

"The people you deal with sound dangerous, Fred. More important, you are letting the house get you with its ghost smell. No honest and earthly business would use the house next door for its home office. Chief Pontiac himself would have shunned that house."

"I don't know if I could have got you in anyway. Don't

tell Blue and Whitey. They'd go along quick enough, even
with Blue's brother being a cop, but they're not smart
enough to handle it. You are my one best brother to confide
in, and Oren, to tell the truth, I don't mind having Latonya
for a buddy. I plan on marrying her and turning honest after
I get my Porsche."

Oren's heart was heavy as he walked into S.S. school. It
wouldn't do him any good to confess to Fred that he had
opened an eye during the ceremony. If Fred knew the danger, it wouldn't slow him down any. Before the ceremony,
Fred had been satisfied with the nickels and dimes he made
on recess bets. Now the house was tempting him with vi-
sions of Porsches. If Oren told Latonya about Fred's deal,
Fred would never trust him again. Who could he tell? What
could he do? Why did he have to spend time in school
when real life demanded so much of his worry time?

Chapter 4

○　○　○

For the month of October, Ms. Pugh's seventh grade class was heavy into Detroit history.

"Pay attention, class. This information will be on our test. A Frenchman by the name of Antoine De La Mothe Cadillac founded Detroit in the year of 1701. That fine man came all the way from France because he knew this was the place where the city of Detroit ought to be, right here where it is on the Detroit River. What was Detroit called in those days? Let me hear it, class."

Over a low mumble from the class, Latonya and Wesley shouted out, "Fort Pontchartrain du Detroit."

Satisfied, Ms. Pugh carried on. "First, the Indians lived here, then the French moved in, after them, the English, after them. . . ."

If there were such a thing as ghosts, Oren seriously doubted if Cadillac's ghost was still hanging around. It was logical to suppose that the French ghosts had long ago cleared out and gone to Canada. Oh, there could be a few no-account, hang-around, leftover fur traders. Fred said the big shot Indian spirits like Pontiac were long gone. Latonya was waving her hand like a madwoman. Before Ms. Pugh granted her permission to speak, Oren knew what she was going to say. Something about ghosts. It was embarrassing, but he and Latonya had the spooky ability to pick up on each other's thoughts, and Oren didn't even want to know what was going on inside Latonya's head.

"Ms. Pugh, as Halloween is coming upon us fast, why don't we combine our Detroit history study with ghosts? It seems to me that the two subjects go together."

"That's a splendid idea, Latonya. We could concentrate on some of the existing historic buildings in the city. Research some of the old houses. In the process we might flush out a ghost or two. It's important for all of us to know about and cherish old Detroit houses."

"Why?" Kimberly Banks asked.

Why was the only word in Kimberly's head, but Ms. Pugh placed high value on Kimberly's "whys."

"You ask, Why?" Ms. Pugh answered thoughtfully. "Detroit's wonderful old houses are getting all boarded up, rejected and neglected, because people move out of Detroit into good-for-nothing, look-alike houses in the suburbs."

"Why?" Kimberly innocently repeated as only she knew how.

"No good reason," Ms. Pugh raged at the whole class like it was them who had said the why. "But a few excuses are given for such moves." Ms. Pugh looked around for a boy or girl who knew more words than Kimberly B. Oren sank in his seat. Latonya waved her hand like the school was on fire, but Ms. Pugh called on Wesley Wrigley Fry, who was a suburban person and must know the answer better.

"People move out of Detroit because they are afraid of being ripped off, mugged, or murdered."

A sensible answer; Oren gave her credit. Old Wesley was shaping up. As her buddy, he had instructed her on how to speak up without whining.

Wesley's explanation angered Ms. Pugh. "Don't people have any courage these days? I have told you children about what the homesteaders in the old West did when wicked cattlemen, evil railroads, or independent riffraff tried to rip them off. Mother, father, and children defended their property. They did not, and I repeat this, they did not take off to some overpriced house in the suburbs with no historic character."

Oren shuddered. Conrad Cord's fist was punching the air for attention. Conrad knew the words to drive Ms. Pugh right up the wall. Who would have thought that Conrad knew how to better than Fred?

"Yes, Conrad?"

"My father and mother intend moving me to the suburbs as soon as they save the money. It will mean a better education for me." Conrad's apple-pie face pleaded for Ms. Pugh to understand.

Ignoring Conrad, Ms. Pugh kept her cool. "I suggest that we start this unit by researching the houses that we now live in. This will mean an exciting class trip to the City-County

Building. I am going to show you how to look up the abstracts on our own Detroit city houses."

"What are abstracts?" Kimberly pushed and strained herself to three words, which was what Ms. Pugh was always encouraging her to do.

"Glad that you asked, Kimberly. Abstracts are records kept in file cabinets."

"My father and mother are going to judge abstract hunting to be a dumb waste of my school time and their tax money," Conrad said. "Besides, my mother says old houses need knocking down."

"You need knocking down, Cord." Fred started to move to get Conrad, but Latonya grabbed onto her buddy's belt and pulled him back. Latonya was careful, because she knew Fred didn't own underwear.

"I live in an apartment project," Blue reminded Ms. Pugh.

Most of the others shared Blue's problem. Fred didn't live any place for sure, and Wesley lived outside the city.

"Oren and Latonya Bell and Dink Bell live in an interesting old house on Fourth Street. I suggest that the class combine their resources to investigate and research the Bell house." Ms. Pugh let them think on that one.

"But we are only renting our house from the city until the expressway wants it." Oren had to say something because Ms. Pugh had accused him of being shy in class discussions.

"All the more reason to get on with it," Ms. Pugh insisted.

"You're all forgetting the house next door to the Bell house," Fred told the class proudly, just like it was his house he was talking about. He spoke correctly, as Ms. Pugh was curing him of the lazy-mouth disease. "I think that house is

just about as old as Oren's house, and I would like to research it by myself with a little help from my buddy,
Latonya Bell. You won't ever have to go inside, Latonya. I
promise."

"Very good, Fred. This project will involve field trips and
personal interviews. We'll need room mothers. Class, we
have a real challenge here. This is what education is all
about."

Ms. Pugh's eyes were flashing. When she was on a roll,
she sucked the whole class in. Oren was on to her. That was
how this teacher worked. Mostly her screwy ideas were
harmless, but dipping into the history of the house next
door was dangerous. Why had Fred brought it up? Fred
didn't know he had opened an eye during the ceremony.
Latonya was waving her hand again.

"Ms. Pugh, for the sake of efficiency, I believe we should
organize into specialty teams. I would like for me and Fred
to be exorcists. I know the house next door has a few nasty
ghosts who need exorcising. Oren and Wesley can head up
the abstract team, as they are in the first reading group.
Blue and Whitey can check the ghosts out on the computers. Dink and the rest of the class can be in general
ghosting."

"Very efficient, Latonya," Ms. Pugh said, "but now it's
time for the band people to go down to the music room."

Wesley fell in beside him when he left the band room. "I
love the way you play third part, Oren," she said sincerely.
"I think you should challenge Dink Bell."

"Wesley, I don't want to sit in the middle seat. I'm the

kind of person who has to be either first or last. I'll challenge Fred when I'm ready."

"That's wise, Oren. Could we read in the library together to practice for our ghost house abstracting? I like that story you were reading to the class about the headless horseman. I can't read and understand all the words to a classic story the way you can."

"I have a comic book at home about the headless horseman," Oren admitted. "But the book has much harder words. You need to stretch yourself above love stories, Wesley."

True to her word, Monday morning Ms. Pugh shifted her historical ghost researchers from S.S. Elementary to the City-County Building in downtown Detroit. His mama took time off from her job to accompany them as a room mother, and his mama worked on an hourly wage. The City-County workers were not as happy to see them show up as Ms. Pugh was to have them be there. Ms. Pugh said if the class all stayed mature, there should be no trouble. Somehow on the way up on the elevator, Latonya lost Fred. He must have slipped off at one of the floor stops. Ms. Pugh didn't blame her, but Latonya knew when she had failed.

While Latonya, Mama, and Ms. Pugh had their heads stuck in file cabinets, Oren, Blue, and Whitey gazed out the window. From up high Detroit was a pretty city, the streets rippling like little ribbons down to the river. The rest of the kids sat at a long table and tried to look mature, but they weren't doing a good job of it.

"Here we go," Latonya screamed. "Alleluia, I found our abstract. I was the first to discover it."

Ms. Pugh congratulated Latonya and took the great abstract to the head of the table for a first reading.

"A Mr. Spiro Spill built the house in the year 1910."

"Seems like I have heard that name before," Wesley said.

Oren knew she never had. He pinched his buddy girl in the arm to help her keep an up-front mouth.

"The name of our school is Spiro Spill Elementary," Ms. Pugh told them. "Isn't that interesting? I believe there is a picture of Mr. Spill in the third-floor hallway. Does anyone remember looking at it?"

No one remembered seeing it. Wesley kept her mouth shut.

"To be honest, I don't remember what the man looks like," Ms. Pugh admitted, "but I believe he left our school a music endowment."

Nobody had any more to say about the name or the picture, so his mama took up the reading of the rest of the abstract. "Spiro Spill, deceased in 1918; his wife, Lotte Spill, deceased in 1918; and their only son, Spiro junior, deceased in 1918."

"Appears there was an unnatural amount of deceasing going on in 1918," Blue remarked. "Maybe we should put it on the computer."

Oren carefully turned the deceasing over in his mind. It must have gone on in the purple bedroom, where the girls slept, because the purple bedroom was closest to the bathroom. A deceasing person would need to be near a bathroom. The facts were adding up. Ms. Pugh was right about how ghosts and history tied in together.

Mama told Conrad Cord to quit banging his head on the table and pay attention. Then she continued to read. "A very long vacancy occurred to the house after the Spills died."

"I guess we can conclude that our house is haunted," Latonya said.

"Oh, no," Dink said. "I wish you wouldn't conclude that, Latonya."

"Face facts, chicken face," Wesley told Dink, and then quickly looked to Oren for approval.

He was doing a better job with Wesley than Latonya was doing with Fred.

"I think we need more facts," Mama said.

"Mama, we have painted the purple bedroom pink and blue, but still the ghostly purple color always bleeds right back through," Latonya pointed out. "And, Mama, Brenda's ghost lives right under my very own bed."

Granddaddy will deny it, Oren thought, *but this time I think that Latonya is onto something.*

"Mrs. Bell is right," Ms. Pugh said. "We need more facts. Tomorrow we will research Spiro Spill."

That night Oren gave Granddaddy a rundown on the abstracting project. Granddaddy kept on coloring his sinking ship and refused Oren his eye, but he chose to say something on the subject.

"What did your abstracting turn up on the house next door?"

"We didn't abstract it out because it was Fred's job to research the house next door, and he didn't stick around long enough."

Should he tell Granddaddy about Fred's business in the house next door? He decided against it. Sometimes, when the spirit of Red Rose was upon him, Bill Bell said more than he ought. What if some day he burped out something about Oren opening an eye during the ceremony? Latonya's ears were always open.

Granddaddy was into ship coloring and appeared to have forgotten the house next door.

Chapter 5

○　○　○

The next morning, Ms. Pugh suggested that the class go down to the end of the hall by twos and take a long look at the picture of Spiro Spill. The class voted on the plan and agreed to do it, but right away they hit a snag. The lights didn't work down at that end of the hall, and there were no windows. Ms. Pugh decided to rouse the janitor, Mr. Thul, who they called Tool because that's how his named sounded.

"Sorry, lady, you need more than a light bulb. The wiring is defective in that wing of the building."

"Couldn't you fix the wiring?" she pleaded, all nice.

"Ain't no classes bein' held down that hall." Tool folded his arms, stubborn to Ms. Pugh's pretty ways.

"Our class wishes to look at the picture on the wall.

Could you take the picture down and bring it into the class-room?"

"I ain't suppose to do nothin' but what is needed for education. Movin' heavy pictures ain't in my contract."

Oren knew Ms. Pugh to be deeply offended by a lazy mouth that offered no hope, but she thanked Tool and then called Mr. Shell, who would do anything for her, and speak correctly while he was doing it. Oren was surprised when Mr. Shell requested him to help out in the big Spiro picture moving. Mr. Shell never chose him for anything in the band room. They walked together down the long, shadowy hall with Oren holding a flashlight and Mr. Shell carrying a lad-der. Mr. Shell told him to direct his light up on the portrait.

"A little higher, old man," Mr. Shell said to Oren.

Oren wasn't an old man, but he didn't mind being called one.

"Ugly son of a gun, isn't he?" Mr. Shell observed.

Oren studied the picture and tried to be fair. "He is not handsome."

"He hangs high and heavy," Mr. Shell said.

Oren held the light steady, but Mr. Shell was having a terrible time doing his part. Spiro didn't want to come down off the dark wall, and when he finally did he nearly took Mr. Shell off the ladder. Also, Spiro was very dirty and spider webbed, and Mr. Shell was wearing a white shirt and dark blue pants. Mr. Shell swore at Spiro and took the Lord's name in vain.

"I hope it wasn't too much trouble." Ms. Pugh smiled.

"No trouble." Mr. Shell lied through his mustache.

Together, Ms. Pugh and Mr. Shell dusted Spiro off and

the class got their first good look at him. Oren wondered why a whole school had been named after such an ugly man.

"Who do you see, class?" Ms. Pugh asked.

Oren didn't want her to think that he was still shy, so he spoke up. "Spiro Spill's not handsome," he said. It was the truth. Mr. Shell had said so before him.

Latonya took insult on his judgment. "Oren, how dare you say Spiro Spill was not handsome? Once upon a time, Spiro's mama gave birth to him, and took pride in what she saw. Now you come along and call that poor lady's child names."

"Oren shouldn't call Spiro Spill names," Dink said in his best Sunday-school voice.

"Spiro Spill was never a handsome man." Wesley supported her buddy. "His nose is beaky. His cap covers his ears, but I bet under his cap his ears are juggy."

"I don't believe he has juggy ears." Dink stood firm.

"You got juggy ears, you chicken head." Fred spit his opinion on Dink's hair and then rubbed it in.

"Spiro Spill was a white person," Blue said.

So far what was noticed was right on. Ms. Pugh encouraged them to continue observing Spiro Spill.

"He has on some kind of uniform," Whitey said.

"This is a dumb waste of my time and the taxpayers' money," Conrad Cord said.

"Maybe he was in the Civil War. The taxpayers won't mind if we study a white man who fought in the Civil War, no matter how ugly he was." Whitey made a good point.

"He is not wearing a military uniform," Mr. Shell said. "I

think he is wearing a band uniform. I find that very interesting. This school does have a music endowment."

"He looks like a loser to me." Fred was more unkind than Oren had been, but Latonya let it pass.

"You are all making wise observations and deductions," Ms. Pugh said, "but I'm afraid we have to give consideration to people like Conrad. Those of us who have an interest in Spiro Spill will have to continue the search on our own time. Will one of you volunteer your home for a meeting?"

Latonya had her hand in the air, and Oren knew where the meeting place would be. It made him uncomfortable to think about all that researching going on in his own home.

Latonya banged on the table for attention. "This is the second meeting of the Spiro Spill Research Team, held on the twenty-first day of October, in the very house on Fourth Street that Spiro built himself, but not actually with his own hands. Wesley, will you please sum up the first meeting. I need to keep my eye on Fred. Brenda Bell, will you get all of your sinking-ship pictures out of the way. Our research team is not into sinking ships."

"Madam Secretary and fellow researchers," Wesley started off. "At the last meeting, Dink Bell resigned because his mother refused to give him permission to go on research hunts or attend meetings. We all agreed that this was no big loss. Mr. Shell had wonderful luck on his assignment. What he found out was the following: Spiro Spill once blew third part trumpet in the John Philip Sousa band, which was the best band in the land in the old days.

By a wonderful coincidence my buddy, Oren Bell, presently plays third part trumpet in the S.S. school band."

"Which is presently the worst band in the land," Granddaddy said.

"We should note," Mr. Shell said, "that when Mr. Spill left the Sousa band, he founded a music studio upstairs in this very house, and more interesting, after his death his will provided a music endowment for the school on Cass Avenue that bears his name. Spiro Spill Elementary has been part of the public school system for many years, and Mr. Spill's special music program is still in existence."

Granddaddy had something to say about that. "Hear this. I blew my silver horn in cities all over this country; small-sized bars, whole-sized halls, speakeasies, blind pigs, outside fields, inside tents and gymnasiums, weddings, and funerals. I sat in with jazz bands and rockabilly bands. I played soul in black churches and blew like Gabriel in uptown churches. I never once heard any talk of this John Philip Sousa group."

"Take my word for it, Bill," Mr. Shell said. "They made a big sound."

"I think at this point,"—Ms. Pugh took over—"we need to piece the story together. Lotte and Spiro were married in 1900, and were, a few years later, part of the John Philip Sousa band's five-year European tour. After that, they left the band and settled down in this good house on Fourth Street and Spiro gave music lessons to the children in the neighborhood. It's time for Fred to say something about his discovery. I do commend Fred, because he did his research by interview."

Fred stood up straight to make his announcement. He

looked taller than usual. "Spiro also built my house. Ms. Pugh and I found out this part through ordinary abstracting. The foundation for the house was dug in 1913. Spiro only intended to live in the Bell flat until he could build himself a real nice house. He had fancy fixings and furniture brought over from Europe, but a big war slowed down the building. The truth is, a successful bootlegger completed the house years after Spiro passed over. This bold bootlegger was knocked off, execution style, inside the house in the late 1930s. I interviewed an old bum in a nursing home on Woodward to get this information, but more than one old bum knows the story. Now, get this. In 1950, three chiropractors set up a clinic, you know where. Soon after, they were robbed and murdered by unknowns. Ms. Pugh and I found this out by reading old newspaper film. Since that time the killer house has been vacant except for bums, winos, freeloaders, and independent adventurers like myself. Once a city inspector ventured inside, but he wasn't alive when he left."

Oren realized that not only were Indians brave and natural musicians, they were also natural researchers. Fred sat down looking mighty proud. Was Fred proud because of his researching, or was he proud because he called the house next door his own?

"Very good, Fred," Ms. Pugh said. "Now, Sarah, what did you find out?"

Oren's mama shifted through her notes and then regarded the research team with sad eyes.

"These are only the bleak, bare-bone facts."

"Tell us, Mama," Latonya urged, "and we will fill in by deducting the details like private eyes do."

"Spiro's problems were duly noted on the society pages of the newspaper because, I suppose, he had money. I don't know if his money came from playing third trumpet or not, but his wife Lotte came from a wealthy Detroit family. This might have been the reason the couple settled in Detroit. Besides our school, Spiro and Lotte donated a wing to old Grace Hospital and they gave money to build up the Congregational Church on Woodward. As Fred pointed out, Spiro built the house next door to our house, but it was never finished and the family never moved in."

"Why wasn't the house ever finished?" Blue said.

Mama looked doubtful, but she continued. "Seems like the men who worked on building the house suffered a series of accidents. A beam fell on one fellow's head. A plasterer broke his legs in a fall. By 1917 our country was at war and Spiro had trouble finding workers to finish the job."

"Was it an accident that killed Spiro?" Latonya asked.

"No," Mama shook her head sadly. "The Spill family caught the 1918 influenza. Lotte and Spiro Jr. died in old Grace Hospital, and Spiro died right here in this house."

"In our purple bedroom—that's where he turned up his toes." Latonya nodded wisely.

"Most probably so," Wesley agreed.

"The family must have caught the sickness from workmen inside the house," Whitey said.

Granddaddy gave out a belch that whiffed the research team with the fumes of Red Rose wine, but his words made sense.

"Sounds to me like this here Spiro was a total loser. He never got to play the first part on any of his Sousa tunes.

His name died out because he had only one sickly son. He wasted his money on schools, hospitals, and churches that gave him no credit for it. He died of an ordinary disease that he took no pleasure from catching. I suspect that his wife Lotte was no beauty."

"The house next door was out to get him, and it got him." Oren summed up the tragedy of Spiro Spill.

"Hey, can I help you draw some sad sinking ships?" Fred asked Brenda. Fred was getting bored with Spiro Spill research.

"Sure," Brenda said.

"I think that we should definitely do something special for Spiro Spill." Ms. Pugh was still fired up for Spiro. "He must have loved Detroit. I found out that he is buried out in old Redford Cemetery on Telegraph Road. Carl"—she smiled at Mr. Shell—"could you arrange some sort of special service for Spiro? His birth date was November first. Halloween, being on a Saturday, would do fine and be a most appropriate time."

"Let Spiro be. Let him be," Granddaddy warned.

"Fred does taps on his trumpet," Mr. Shell said. "The Friday before Halloween, the S.S. band will have its first concert. It could be a memorial concert. It could be a memorial concert for Spiro. After performing in the S.S. auditorium, we could take our music to the cemetery."

"Could the band play a John Philip Sousa number?" Ms. Pugh asked.

"No," Mr. Shell sighed. "The only numbers that the S.S. band knows how to play are the London Bridge Overture and variations of 'Twinkle, Twinkle Little Star.'"

"The London Bridge Overture and variations of 'Twinkle' will do fine," Ms. Pugh said. "I wish we had the funds available to transport the class to the Redford Cemetery on Halloween. Old cemeteries are so historical."

"Hearing the S.S. band play won't do a thing for the remains of Spiro Spill, but it might give the house next door a good laugh," Granddaddy said.

Fred stopped drawing on his sinking ship and took charge. "Ms. Pugh, if you want us to perform a concert for a ghost at a cemetery, this is how we do it. We charge a buck a ticket for our school concert. We take the proceeds and finance a big wake at McDonald's for Spiro and the Seventh grade. We don't need transportation. It's no trick to hitch a ride on Telegraph Road. Might have to put two kids on a corner, but four kids at a gas station would ride slick and quick."

Mr. Shell could see that Ms. Pugh didn't like Fred's idea, so he came up with one of his own. "Since the grave performance would be on a Saturday, I could get a bus from my high school and drive it myself. We'd need permission slips."

"That's a better idea," Latonya said. "I could never hitch a ride lugging Sousa. Here's another nit to worry over. Aunt Grace won't give Dink permission to go inside a graveyard, and he plays the all-important medium trumpet part. Another worry. I could lose Fred, and he plays the all-important first part."

"I know nothing about music and this may be a stupid thought," Mama said, "but as Spiro played third trumpet in his band and Oren plays third trumpet in the S. S. Elementary band, it seems to me that Oren has the most important part in a memorial concert for Spiro."

"You're right, Sarah," Granddaddy said. "You don't know anything about music and that was a stupid thought."

Fred was peevish because Ms. Pugh liked one of Mr. Shell's ideas better than one of his, so he thought up another one to put him ahead.

"If the art department draws up some posters to advertise our school concert, well, then I'll personally place them in places of business along Cass Avenue, Third Street, and Woodward."

"Most of those places of business are dirty-book stores," Blue reminded Fred.

Ms. Pugh jumped in to make Fred's idea respectable. She hated to see him put down or cut out.

"I think it's an excellent idea for the art department to be involved in the project, and university students and professors pass by those places of business."

Granddaddy chuckled. "Students, professors, winos, hookers, and punks—who among them will pay a buck to listen to the worst band in the land?"

It was late when the meeting was over, so Wesley's mama, Ms. Pugh, and Mr. Shell drove all the kids home, except Fred. Fred refused to be driven, and it was hard to talk Fred out of a refusal. He said his new foster mama lived close by and he wanted to walk. Latonya wanted him to stay the night and not pass by the house next door in the dark. Fred claimed that he had the house under perfect control. Oren walked Fred out on the front porch. They eyeballed the dome on the Fisher Building, but not for long. Fred wasn't into staring at beautiful buildings.

"Oren, I can still get you in. My boss likes kids to do the

running. The steamer operation is now my main thing. I've been promoted. I'm more than just a delivery boy. I made a real contact today and made myself a hundred bucks. My contact was a harmless foot doctor. His secretary told me to be seated and the doctor would be with me in a minute. He was glad to see me. The poor guy needed some relief from payments on his Caddie. I felt good offering him the relief. I don't have a thing to do with the car heisting. How about it, Oren? Want in?"

"No, thank you."

He watched Fred disappear in the dark direction of the house next door. Maybe living with Latonya and Mama was making Oren too pickie honest. If the deal weren't tied in with the house next door, he might consider it.

"Oren Bell, will you carry yourself back inside this house on the double. We have a serious family crisis." Latonya sounded more fussed than usual.

He carried himself back inside. "What's the crisis?"

"Brenda Bell, repeat to Oren what you told Mama and me and Granddaddy too."

"Oren, Mr. Figment is Spiro Spill and Spiro Spill is Mr. Figment. They are one in the same ghost. Isn't that good news?"

Mama came in sternly. "Brenda, I thought you understood that Mr. Figment is a figment of your imagination."

"He is my best friend in the whole world."

"Brenda, how do you know that Mr. Figment is Spiro Spill?" Oren tried for some common sense.

"I always knew that my friend was the man who built our house and the evil house next door. I didn't know his name before. Thank you, guys, for finding out his real name for me. He wouldn't tell me himself because I think he forgot."

Oren asked Granddaddy what he thought.

"Don't think it makes a damn bit of difference what Brenda calls her ghost," Bill Bell grumbled.

Mama must have agreed with Granddaddy because she started shooing them off to bed. Granddaddy went along with her shooing. Oren knew Bill had a bottle of Red Rose stashed in his bottom drawer, not to mention a carton of cigs. Bill Bell wasn't allowed to smoke in bed, but he did.

Oren offered to read Brenda and her ghost their bedtime story. First off, Brenda wanted to show him all her sad, sinking, or sunken ships. The year before, Brenda had been crazy about kangaroos, although she never saw more than a picture of one. This year she was into sunken and sinking ships. That was the way of Brenda. She was a weird little kid.

"Look, Oren, I found these books by myself in the library. I checked them out by myself. It was easy. I get to keep them three weeks and then I renew."

"Neat, Brenda."

They were grown-up books. One book was called *Shipwrecks of the Great Lakes,* and the other book, *Shipwrecks of the Seven Seas.*

"Brenda, do you read these books?"

"No, the words are too hard. I use them mostly to get real names for my sunken ships. Granddaddy helps me do the lettering."

Oren picked up Fred's drawing. It looked like an upside down Rub-a-dub-dub, three men in a tub. He looked at one of Granddaddy's drawings. It looked like a plunging cigar.

"Brenda, did Granddaddy and Fred get their ship names out of your books?"

"No, Granddaddy and Fred don't draw real ships. They make up their own names."

He studied Granddaddy's sinking ship. The name had been lettered carefully on the bow or front of the plunging cigar in black crayon, while numbers were penciled in fine print inside the body of the funny-looking boat. Fred's up-side-down tub was even more weird. It had three little stick men falling out of it. They had squares attached to their legs. Blocks of cement, Oren guessed. Fred was a better artist than Granddaddy. He had drawn in what looked like part of the Detroit river and riverfront with a spot discon-nected from the land. It didn't look to be an island meant for good times like Belle Isle. It was a dark, polluted spot located downriver, so it must be Zug Island. Granddaddy and Fred doodled while they were drawing ships. He won-dered why they doodled specific names and numbers; but then, doodles were private thoughts that belonged to the artist.

"See by the window, Oren. Spiro is waiting for the story. Start reading. Read to us about sinking and sunken ships."

He couldn't see Spiro. He sighed and started to read.

"The *Waubona* was a little sidewheeler making her last run of the year." Oren shuddered because he knew what always happened to Brenda's ships. Doomed ships were like doomed houses. While one ship could leave port and get its travelers safely across the lake, the very same storm would settle one of Brenda's ships to the bottom of the lake where the cursed boat would take up space forever and become haunted. Unlucky ships and houses should be left alone.

Chapter 6

○   ○   ○

Frequently, when the house heating bill outgrew Mama's paycheck, hocking Granddaddy's silver horn came up at family conferences. Granddaddy always vetoed the proposal and the horn stayed safely under the living room sofa. Now here was Latonya actually insisting that Granddaddy lend his horn to Oren for the concert. Oren knew blame well that he didn't deserve the silver horn, and he dreaded the ill feelings bound to spark out in all directions when Granddaddy refused to give it to him.

"I freely do admit, Oren is a boy and therefore my favorite grandchild, but he cannot blow my silver horn, even one single time. The boy sits last chair trumpet in the worst band in the entire land."

"Mama," Brenda reported for spite, and because she loved to tattle, "Granddaddy sneaked over to the house next door this morning to drink Red Rose wine. He wouldn't be talking so smart now if he hadn't napped all afternoon."

"Shut your face, Brenda," Latonya warned.

It was news to Oren that Granddaddy went inside the house next door, so it must be news to Latonya. Most times, Latonya would come down hard on Granddaddy for such dallying, but now she needed him to be mellow.

Mama looked from face to face, trying to figure where to aim her support. She always appreciated the feelings of all sides in family arguments, and this slowed down her decisions.

"Latonya," she implored, "tell me again. Why does Oren have to play Granddaddy's horn?"

"You know the story, Mama. You said it yourself. Oren has the all-important third part to play."

Granddaddy leaped in on this point. "Oren is presently playing Spiro's horn. The research team deducted and accepted this for fact. Let Oren continue to play Spiro's horn."

"Oh, Granddaddy," Latonya wailed, "Spiro's horn needs to be retired. S.S. students have banged it around for years. The valves are loose, some lost, and Mr. Shell doesn't know where to find them. Mama, make Granddaddy lend Oren his horn for the concert and taps at the cemetery. I agree that Oren is a terrible musician, but my twin brother is a careful person."

"Listen here, Missy Latonya," Granddaddy snapped

back. "Spiro Spill was well satisfied with being dead until you and Ms. Peeyoo stirred him up."

"Oh, yeah? Then why is he still hanging around our purple bedroom?" Latonya had him there.

Granddaddy had to think on that one for a time, because he did have respect for Brenda's weird notions and ghost sightings. He shrugged and came up with his final word on the subject.

"If I let any member of the S.S. band blow my silver horn, it would be Fred, but I don't intend letting him blow it either. So forget it. I do not endorse the S.S. band."

Mama put up her hand to show that she had come to a decision.

"If Granddaddy judges our Oren to be unqualified to blow his horn, then so be it. Such a noble instrument as the trumpet of Spiro Spill must have one more good blow left in it."

"Mama," Brenda began to plead, "Latonya intends to drive Spiro away from our purple room with her exorcising. She intends doing it after taps is blown. Please Mama, don't let Latonya exorcise my ghost away."

"Spoiled, mean, selfish girl," Latonya said. "Spiro needs to be with his own kind."

"Brenda Bell," Mama said, "Spiro doesn't talk to me. I don't know if he wants to stay or go. You'll have to work that one out with Latonya."

Oren was relieved that he didn't have to use Granddaddy's horn. Still, he had to perform in the school concert, and play taps for Spiro. He was committed. He knew in his heart that he did not have the skill to carry out either assignment. He wasn't the only one worrying over the concert.

Mr. Shell was offering false hope to Ms. Pugh that the two concerts would be a success. He swore at the band when Ms. Pugh wasn't around, but swearing at them didn't improve the sound of the London Bridge Overture or variations of "Twinkle Twinkle." Desperate to make the program work, Mr. Shell had given his star, Latonya Bell, a solo part on Sousa, whose real name turned out to be sousaphone. Latonya had stepped up on her practicing, and Granddaddy had taken to disappearing before supper. Oren worried over the direction his Granddaddy was taking, but he didn't know what to do about it.

With Bill Bell gone in the evening, Oren felt free to pick up Spiro's old horn and start playing along beside Latonya and Sousa. Brenda knew all the parts, so she accompanied them on her song flute. Mama said they made nice music together, but Oren doubted that this was true.

The tickets kept selling. A concert for a ghost caught the attention of all sorts of people. Fred didn't hit all of the practices, but he was doing PR work for the band all up and down Cass Avenue. Mama had been talking around the J. L. Hudson Company, and Wesley Wrigley Fry's mama put the word out in her suburb.

The S.S. auditorium always gave Ms. Pugh a thrill. Newer schools settled for multipurpose rooms, but old S.S. had a stage, lights, and seats like a movie theater. The night of the concert the S.S. auditorium was filled to the limit. It was a real first in the history of the school. The band fund was overflowing with money. Mr. Shell had covered himself by filling out the S.S. band with members of his Northwestern High School band. A tall, cool trumpeter with a chin beard sat between Oren and Dink, taking Fred's first part because Fred had disappeared, which was Latonya's fault. The biggest horn took up so much of her time that she had neglected her duty to Fred.

Mr. Shell walked on stage, handsome in a ruffled shirt and velvet suit. He bowed to the audience. Then, as he was big on bowing, he bowed to the band. He lifted his baton and brought it down hard, like it was the baton that was turning on the music. The London Bridge Overture swelled from wall to wall. By the time the band reached Latonya's solo, the audience seemed to be with them all the way, but Oren had the good sense not to relax when things were going good. While Latonya played, he held his breath and prayed. She played the melody of London Bridge like she had a million times before, missing a note here and there, but not so many that anybody except Mr. Shell would notice. Oren exhaled his breath and filled his lungs with new air. She was done with it. Mr. Shell bowed to Latonya. She stood up in order to bow back to him. Then Latonya threw up all over the floor. By the funny, dazed look in his eyes, Oren feared that Mr. Shell had lost his wits. After a long minute the bandmaster recovered himself and signaled the Northwestern fill-ins to start playing what the S.S. band knew to be the Washington Post March by John Philip Sousa. Oren and Dink blew right along beside the tall, whiskered trumpeter, not able to hear themselves play or know for sure what it was they were playing, but still smartly keeping up. The rest of the band measured up and did the same. Mr. Tool marched onstage to the music, his overalls and pail a funny sight next to Mr. Shell's fancy suit and baton. The custodian bowed to the band and the audience and to Mr. Shell, and then proceeded to mop up the mess in front of Latonya before somebody slipped in it and broke his neck. Oren had to give credit to old Tool. He mopped to the beat. The number came to a cymbal-clashing finish, with Wesley Wrigley Fry going wild on drums. The band stood up and bowed then, and the audience clapped, but Oren seriously doubted if the people got a dollar's worth of pleasure out of the concert.

All the way home, Aunt Grace kept repeating to Mama, "What happened to poor Latonya?" She had the sense to shut up when they went by the house next door.

Granddaddy wasn't home yet. Mama decided to lock him out for the night, him not being trustworthy enough for his own key. The Bell house rule required all Bells to be in by ten o'clock. Oren pleaded to give Granddaddy more time, but Mama held her ground.

"It's not November yet, Oren. Your Granddaddy has himself winterized with enough booze to withstand a few chill winds."

Too wound up for sleep, Oren settled down on the sofa. During the concert, he had offered up a brief prayer for Latonya. For his effort, his only twin sister was branded forever as the girl who threw up during a concert. Granddaddy was left outdoors to freeze. Brenda was crying because it was her last night with Spiro Spill. The following morning he, Oren Bell, was committed to blowing Spiro home without the help of the Northwestern band, and most likely not Fred's help either. It was a humiliating year for the Bell family.

* * *

The Northwestern band was invited to go along to do a follow-up on the S.S. trumpet section's performance of taps. Fred actually showed up, and Aunt Grace gave Dink permission to do his medium best. Oren was glad for all the innocent dead people who weren't able to get up and walk off if the music made them sick. All the way to the old Redford Cemetery, there was whooping up and making out on the school bus. The Northwestern band was not as disciplined or stylish as Mr. Shell claimed. Oren sat quietly in his seat and worried. Granddaddy was still out on the town. Sometimes Granddaddy went to sleep in an all-night movie and it took the cops a while to find him.

On first landing at the cemetery, Mr. Shell collected his S.S. trumpet section and took them off beyond Ms. Pugh's hearing.

"Listen to me, Fred Lightfoot," Mr. Shell said to Fred's indifferent ear. "You do not deserve to be so talented on the horn, but by some miracle you are. It is time that you put your talent to use. If you take off before you blow Spiro Spill's ghost home, thereby breaking Ms. Pugh's heart, Spiro will team up with an ancient Indian curse and get you. No escape. Fred Lightfoot will disappear forever. Splat. Poof. No proof. Understand?"

"Sure, sure, I understand," Fred said.

Mr. Shell stationed his taps trio in different spots around the cemetery, placing Oren by himself behind the tombstone of Horatio Gray, who had been dead since 1897.

"Listen, Oren, old man, Fred will do the first part, over behind the big oak tree on the Telegraph Road side. As I explained to Dink, once in a while we all have to depend on an undependable person. Now is one of those times. Oren, listen for Fred to play taps all the way through. On Fred's last note, you'll hear Dink pick it up on the north corner of the cemetery. Oren, you wait till Dink's last note; and then carefully lift it up on the count and take off. Do the best you can. Dink and Fred will join you on your last note, and the three of you will blow Spiro home together. Make it beautiful for Spiro and Ms. Pugh."

"I'll try," Oren promised Mr. Shell. Eager to get Spiro's dishonor over with, he leaned against Horatio's tombstone and waited. Finally, he heard Fred's horn moaning sad and clear through the autumn air. Fred reached a high note and held it, then let it down easy like soft falling rain. How could he do it? It was a miracle. Dink came in from the north, not fancy, but enough. Oren took a deep breath and brought Spiro's very own trumpet to his lips. He cleared his mind of thoughts concerning the house next door and Granddaddy. Not forgetting the loose valves, he held the horn tight so it wouldn't fall apart while he played. Right on. The old horn did have a few sweet notes left. Suddenly Fred and Dink were with him, all three of them blowing Spiro home as one. The living and the dead in old Redford Cemetery held a long moment of reverent silence, then with a mighty drum roll from Wesley Wrigley Fry, the Northwestern High–Spiro Spill Elementary band exploded into the Washington Post March.

All that remained was the hamburger wake at McDonald's, and they had plenty of money for it.

When they arrived home, Granddaddy's snoring body blocked the front door. Latonya kicked him. He sat up and said, "Oren Bell can't play my horn."

Latonya insisted that they had immediate business in the purple bedroom. She suspected that Spiro Spill still lurked there, even though the band had given him a grand send-off. She was right. She perceived his aura coming out of a corner. Brenda admitted that he was there. Oren wished he had the knack of seeing Spiro.

"Brenda Bell, you are Spiro's number-one girl. He won't go away, not for the band or for me or for Fred. You do it, girl. Spiro deserves to be set free."

Brenda tearfully agreed. She jumped on the bed three times and chanted "I love you, Spiro Spill." Then she sat quiet and calmly repeated an exorcist's verse.

Come out of the corners
of this old purple room.
Free yourself, Spiro
and go zoom, zoom, zoom.

They waited.

"He won't go, Latonya." Brenda sighed.

"Don't fret, Brenda." Latonya patted Brenda's head. "He'll go when he's ready. We freed him to do so."

Oren eased his body around the lumps and exposed springs in the sofa. Just when a person accepted probable disaster, the situation turned out right for no explainable reason. Fair was fair and credit should be given where it was due. His prayers actually starting to hold the house off. He had better give the Lord one for thanks.

71

"Dear Lord,
Thanks
for Granddaddy making it home safe
for Fred not taking off when we needed him
for Spiro staying on to comfort Brenda
for Dink and me playing on key when we never did
before.
Good work. Keep trying, Lord.
Your friend, Oren Bell."

Chapter 7

o   o   o

Oren opened the back door and bowed from his
waist to welcome Skid, the grand old cat. Must
have been six months since he'd last seen
Skid, but he wasn't surprised. The first frost
brought old Skid out of the alley. Skid had wintered in the
Spill–Bell house before the Bells moved in. He had been
there to greet them the first day they opened the front door,
and he especially appreciated it when they turned on the
heat. Skid had stretched himself out in front of the heat
register, and soaked the warmth into his fur like he was
enjoying love for the first time. Spring fever took Skid back
to the alley and streets, but the Bells were happy to welcome him back when his free life turned cold. Now Skid
moved confidently past Latonya's legs into his old spot be-

neath the ancient, high-legged stove. Latonya, busy with her winter soup pot, stooped to give him a pat.

"Here you go, you nasty old cat, a chicken liver that I've been saving for you. Listen, Oren, go upstairs and see if Aunt Grace has any helpings for the pot."

Latonya scraped every last piece of anybody's leftovers into her pot on the back burner, where the stuff simmered from the first of November until the last day of March. Her soup tasted better than garbage after it cooked awhile, even though it was garbage. When the old furnace kicked out, Latonya's pot heated the flat.

"Aunt Grace received her aid check today, so it's steak night for the upstairs Bells. Get going, Oren."

"You know, Latonya, the upstairs Bells have a new protection—a German shepherd by the name of Fritz. Fritz has papers to prove he's pure highbred. That puts Fritz first in line for accepting steak bones."

"Time yourself on the button and grab one of Fritz's bones. I dumped too much cabbage in the pot yesterday and my soup needs a bone to lighten the flavor."

Oren didn't intend to take a bone away from a protection dog, so he brought up a new subject. "Latonya, I need serious help with my long division. I know how to do them well enough, but I always get the wrong answer. Blue says that his brother says the Detroit police department has calculator machines doing their long-division work. Blue says learning long division is a big waste of time. Even so, I'll learn long division, if you help me."

"Let Fred help you."

"Fred is too busy to help me."

"Let Brenda help you."

Oren sulked down low at this suggestion. Latonya knew full well how he hated having his little sister help him with math, even though Brenda was the queen of arithmetic in the Bell house. Very weird and unnatural, watching an eight-year-old girl push numbers around a page, forcing them to give up the right answer. It was sort of like the way that Fred knew how to divide percentages in his head, and hit a high note on the trumpet.

"Seems to me, Oren Bell," Latonya said, "that you should be proud to have a number genius for a little sister. I've called on Brenda for help plenty of times, of course, not as many as you. It's getting late. You go hunt Brenda up. There are reports of mean-looking strangers hanging around the house next door. Aunt Grace says that's the reason why she decided to add Fritz to her family, but that dog avoids the sight of the house next door. Puts his tail between his legs when Aunt Grace makes him look at it. Dogs know. Smack Brenda for wandering off. I give you permission to do so."

Oren agreed to find Brenda. He worried over his little sister's boldness. She knew better than to go near the house next door, but she was unpredictable. He scooted across the field, and then slowed down when he came to the rotting steps. Brenda might go inside the house, but not him. It was not yet half past six, but the sun was going down and the shadows would soon be out. The sound of inward stirrings mocked his ears. Fred said rats as big as dogs went about their business inside and around the house. Oren called out cautiously, "Brenda Bell."

"I'm right here, Oren." The sound of her voice was not inside, not outside. Where?

"Brenda Bell," he called again softly, so as not to wake the dangers that slept through the day.

"Right here," Brenda piped again.

This time his ear traced her voice to the crawl space under the decayed porch.

"What are you doing under the porch, Brenda? Are you caught on something?"

"No, I'm waiting for you, Oren. Come down under here and get us both out. We need rescuing."

Oren peering under a broken board, trying to adjust his eyes to the darkness in order to make out Brenda's problem. If she had company, he sure hoped that it was Spiro Spill. Brenda sat on a pile of rags, the head of an animal in her lap. It had glassy eyes and short hair. At first Oren thought his little sister had hold of a big rat, but then he saw it was a small dog that looked like a rat.

"Brenda Bell!" he raged at her in relief.

"Don't you be provoked with me, Oren. Help me get Buttercup home."

"Skid came back today," he warned her. "You know how that old cat hates dogs. Skid will kill the poor sick hound you've got there."

Oren eased himself under the sagging boards. Brenda scrambled out nimble and quick, giving him room to solve her problem. In the darkness, he sized the situation up by feel of hand. What Brenda had here was an expecting mother dog whose time was soon to come upon her. The dog seemed good-natured enough. Oren gently picked the mother dog up in his arms, then like a bent-over acrobat juggling a sack of eggs, he pushed and slipped himself and the dog to the surface. Brenda and the dog kissed him. The cold November wind froze their kisses to his face.

"I love you, Oren Bell," Brenda told him. "Granddaddy wouldn't help me. He's sitting inside that wicked house right now drinking his Red Rose wine."

Oren thought about giving Granddaddy a holler before taking Brenda home. Granddaddy would never answer a holler. The dark was moving in fast. Better to deliver Brenda and her dog to Latonya for safekeeping, then go back for Granddaddy. Latonya would give the dog some soup, smack Brenda, and clear the way for him to get Granddaddy to bed. It saddened Mama to come home from working hard all day and see Granddaddy stupefied. Holding fast to the bulging beagle, Oren instructed Brenda to grip his coat for the trip across the vacant field to safety.

"You better play the long-division game with me later, Brenda Bell," he told her sternly. "Quick, go inside and get the flashlight for me. You know where it is."

Retrieving Granddaddy from inside the house next door was going to take more courage than he actually possessed, but he had to do it. He knew Bill Bell only wanted an abandoned place for uninterrupted drinking, but some of the steamer men might get sight of him and think he was a witness. A witness to any crime was a dangerous person to be. A good rule to remember while performing a frightful duty is: keep your brain steady on neutral, lest fearful thoughts creep in and take over. He walked up the steps and faced the front door of the house. It was thick and locked. From the sidewalk he had always imagined the door knocker to be a shrunken head, but common sense told him up close it would look different. It didn't. The wrinkles were carves in the wood, but sure enough, was a head. He knew there were loose boards on the basement windows, but his Granddaddy wouldn't have entered by sliding through a window. It wasn't his style. Bill Bell walked through doors, so there had to be an unlocked door. There was a glass-and-cement-block room stuck on the back of the house. He'd try that. He walked cautiously around to the side of the house that faced his own home. The light in his kitchen window offered him the comforting sight of Latonya's head. It occurred to him that the house had a full view of their family doings, because the Bells never thought to pull their shades against an empty house. He was walking steady and making good progress, when suddenly something snaked out and grabbed his ankle, pulling him down in the weeds. He lay still, making a mighty effort to collect his wits. He sat up, his brain on steady neutral, and made a careful inspection. A tree growing strong under the weeds had done it. He had to be more heedful, never forgetting that the weeds and wild-growing trees belonged to the house and must do its bidding. He was right about there being a glass door on the glass room. He put his hand through the jagged cut in the door, knowing that the house would cut him if he gave it the chance. The inside knob turned easily, and Oren was sure this was the way his Granddaddy had gained entrance to the house. He flashed his light around the room. No Granddaddy. His mama had done some guessing as to what this room had been used for, seeing as how their house didn't have one like it. She figured it might have been a plant room, and then later a waiting room for the chiropractors. There was a sofa and chairs and piles of old magazines. He thought about taking some of the old-time magazines home to Mama and the girls, but then decided against it. Let the house keep what belonged to it.

His feet crunched broken glass as he went on his way through the door to the next room. Fred had told him the layout of the house was sort of like his own house, but with more and bigger rooms. The room leading to the kitchen must be an eating room, but not a regular dining room. He played his light on the walls. Figures of fancy, faded red ladies and gentlemen in a withered garden mocked him with their dim, dead smiles. People trapped in old wallpaper didn't worry him, so he moved bravely into the kitchen. Standing in the middle of the kitchen, his neutral brain took everything in. The big old refrigerator was from the same time zone as the one Latonya used, but this one was bigger and grander. No doubt about it, this house made too much of itself. A wonder that the flashy old refrigerator hadn't had its hinges ripped off. Something funny. The refrigerator was moaning. It was turned on. How could that be? Another sound! Sounded like something he'd heard before. He listened. The heart of the noise was the Washington Post March, but not played in perfect time like it had been by the Northwestern High School band. The notes and rests made a scratching and echoing sound. He followed the eerie music into the center hallway, and then into the front parlor. A large piece of furniture with a big horn on top was painfully cranking out the beat to the phantom march. Bill Bell was stretched out on a long leather couch, listening to the tinny old music and babbling to himself.

"That's the way horns and drums should sound."

Granddaddy was out, but he still had some talk programmed in him to come out. It looked like he had been burning something in the fireplace. Did the chimney work? Oren picked his grandfather up in his arms. Bill Bell was light enough for a strong boy to carry, and he gave no resistance. It was like holding a sack full of bird bones. Oren dropped the flashlight. The beam went out. He put Granddaddy down for a time to look for the flashlight, but he couldn't find it. He picked up the human pile of rags again. His Granddaddy didn't feel any too alive, but Bill Bell was still talking and breathing low. Better get him home quick. There was still a glint of dirty grayness from the window. The hallway was black. He forgot where the doors were located, and a wall blocked his progress like cold rock. He stopped to collect his wits. There it was. He smelled the ghost smell. Fred was right about the smell. It was faint and whiffy, not out to hit you right on, but it smelled a million times worse than any puke alive when it finally got inside his nose and lungs. Spiro was not the one haunting this house. Spiro was a clean ghost. Keep his brain and nose on neutral, and by trial and error he could find the glass room and the way out. Enough gray light in the breakfast room to see the fast-fading red figures, but mercifully their fake smiles were masked by the shadows. Finally he felt the crushed glass of the last room under his feet. He cut his hand opening the door, and had to put his Granddaddy down for a minute to wipe the blood on his duckie shirt. Bill Bell belched. Oren knew his grandfather was alive and nearly home safe. It was finished. He had rescued his Granddaddy from the house.

Halfway across the vacant field, he put Granddaddy

down in order to give his scare-strained muscles a break. Granddaddy had started up again, mumbling his rambling Red Rose thoughts, all about what a lousy horn player his only grandson was. How was Oren going to keep Granddaddy from going back inside the house? Bill Bell was stubborn on having his own way, and he didn't have the sense left to be afraid of danger. Oren turned and studied the house next door. Outlined against the evening sky, there was a smug pride about the sagging, stinking old ruin. He wasn't afraid of it. He had gone in and come out. That was better than walking backward past it with his eyes closed.

"Old house, you had better not come on to Bill Bell no more or give our family any hard luck. You had better stop blighting up our neighborhood. You had better not tempt Fred with your dirty deals. Your evil powers are all nincompoopery."

Then he gave the house a straightforward finger. It was a little bit foolish and a lot dangerous to curse a house of bad reputation, but he felt brave as an Indian while doing it. Was the face of the house changing? Early night was its best time for looking mean. One long red eye was flickering a response to his curse. He knew there was some power turned on inside the house because of the refrigerator. Had there been somebody else in the top of the house, while he was crashing around below? He picked up Granddaddy and made a dash for the warmth of his own house. Even Spiro Spill had the sense to do his haunting safe inside the home the Bells had made their own, and he was the one who had built the house next door.

Latonya held the door open and cleared the way. Oren bolted straight through to Granddaddy's room and dumped him on the bed. He checked to make sure he was still breathing, covered him up, and then closed the door on his way out so the deadly Red Rose fumes wouldn't penetrate the rest of the house. He ambled out to the kitchen to see how Latonya and Brenda were managing the animals.

Shifting Skid, the girls had made a cozy bed for Buttercup under the stove. Latonya said Skid's ornery spirit seemed subdued by his season in the alley. He had relocated himself on top of the leaning old refrigerator. Mama entered to this settled and homey sight. It gave her pause to smile. She accepted Skid's return, and agreed to extend a helping hand to the mother dog in her time of need. Ignoring Granddaddy's empty chair, Mama sat down to warm herself with a bowl of Latonya's soup. Oren knew himself to be responsible for a large portion of the contentment in the kitchen.

Buttercup became pet to the girls, while Skid took charge of Oren and Granddaddy. During the day, Skid centered himself on Granddaddy's lap, leaving that spot only once a day to do his outdoor business. Skid's brief absence did not give Granddaddy enough time to sneak off next door, so Bill Bell stayed home. Bill didn't mind offending people, but he hated to offend old cats. Oren decided not to bring up the subject of the house.

For eight blessed days, Oren came home from school to find his grandfather full of nothing but Latonya's soup. At night, while the house slept, Skid crept in beside Oren. It was a wonder how clean an old alley cat knew to keep his person. The steady hum of the old cat's purr was fine music to go to sleep by. Most remarkable of all, Skid honored the mother dog by giving her first turn at the animal soup bowl. The folks upstairs made fun of Buttercup's appearance. Aunt Grace predicted that they would all come down with cancer or worse by touching the old cat and mother dog. Granddaddy said that, as Fritz was a purebred idiot, the upstairs Bells were in danger of catching a mental disease from the foolish beast.

The morning of the big long-division test, Skid left Oren's side before daylight. Feeling cold from the separation, Oren followed the cat to the kitchen. Located over the furnace and steaming with soup heat, the kitchen offered more warmth than the rest of the house. Wow! Oren wondered over the miracle he saw under his own stove. Buttercup had divided herself into nine small, squeaking brand-new dogs. Did the city of Detroit need nine more hound dogs? Buttercup smiled at him with her tongue hanging out, like she had done something to be petted over. Skid paced and wailed, guarding the new babies and warning human hands to keep away. Oren decided to wake up the family, so they could view the wonderful sight together.

The first day after the birth of the puppies, Latonya accepted advance orders. Not everyone qualified to be a puppy parent. She had placed all but one of the pups by the second week. Conrad Cord begged for the last pup.

"Latonya, I'm moving soon to a northwest Detroit house in a safe neighborhood with a big backyard. I'll feed my pup dog food out of a can. I'll present you with a signed permission slip from my mother."

"I just don't know, Conrad. Those favors you mention for dogs have been overrated. A dog needs more than a big backyard, dog food out of a can, and permission from a mother."

"What then? What? I'll give my pup what it needs, Latonya. I promise. Tell me, what does it need?"

"A dog needs a sense of work. Even Fritz Bell guards our house in his own stupid way. The pup I promised to the fire station will get training on helping out and cheering up firemen. Wesley Wrigley Fry's daddy intends taking Wesley's pup out to jog with him each morning. Wesley's daddy is a Ford executive, and that busy man could drop of a heart attack, if he didn't have a lively pup to go jogging with him."

"I'll give my pup jobs to do, Latonya," Conrad pledged. "My pup can pick up my socks off the floor, but only if you think that sock picking up is a good job for a dog."

"Think up better jobs, Conrad, and I'll erase the definite no after your name, and put in a maybe."

Each day brought exciting puppy progress. Their eyes opened and they saw the light. Their bellies grew fat on Buttercup's milk. Latonya proclaimed a celebration, and made her famous no-egg cake on the day the pups started taking their first steps.

After dinner on no-egg cake day, the smallest pup in the litter separated herself from the rest. She wobbled on her new walking legs in small circles, making age-old dog howls. By ten o'clock she still circled, pleading her trouble. Granddaddy, Mama, Oren, Latonya, Brenda, Skid, and Buttercup watched with alarm. By midnight the puppy had taken herself across the room away from her brothers and sisters. With one last hopeless circle, she dropped. There was no denying it. She just dropped dead. Oren had seen dead animals before, mostly discarded homeless carcasses, killed by violent wickedness, accident, or neglect. This little animal, all loved and spoken for, had died before their caring eyes and there was nothing to do for it.

Brenda had given each pup a name and knew one from the other. The name of the dearly departed happened to be Sharkie Sue Bell. While the rest of the pups securely nursed close to Buttercup, Oren hunted up a shoe box for Sharkie Sue's remains. The Bells parted for the night, too tired for words. Granddaddy slept in the living room chair. Skid slid in beside Oren on the sofa. From the purple room, Oren heard Brenda's high little voice singing her night song.

Sharkie Sue, oh, Sharkie Sue
all brand new
God took you back before you grew.
I wanna know. I wanna know
where do angel puppies go?

"That Brenda," Granddaddy chuckled. "She sure smarts it over the rest of us. She jingles words around and uses numbers like other kids play with toys from K mart. By the way, Oren, what did you get on your last math test? I don't remember you saying."

"I received a seventy-eight, Granddaddy."

"Seventy-eight? I told you to study."

"I did."

"My God, Oren, I'd understand if you got ten percent to, say, fifty percent right. Us Bell men often show our contempt for tests by flunking them. I'd rejoice if you took a ninety or one hundred, because us Bell men know how to achieve when it pleases us to do so, but a seventy-eight borders on dangerously medium. I'd expect Grace's boy, Fink, to get a seventy-eight."

"Seventy-eight adds up to a C plus, Granddaddy. Dink received a seventy-five, which is an on-target C."

"Medium plus does not cut it in life. Oren, now that the runt is dead, I sincerely hope that the rest of the pups keep healthy and hold on. I don't take well to misery."

Oren's last thoughts before sleep were of the house next door. Buttercup had come from there. If Latonya knew how he had failed on the ceremony, and how he had taunted the house . . . if she knew she wouldn't think the pup's death was natural. No use to worry her over it. No use to talk to Granddaddy. Nothing to be gained by talking to Fred. Mama would listen to him, but he didn't want to worry her. It was his burden to bear and he would have to deal with it alone.

Chapter 8

○   ○   ○

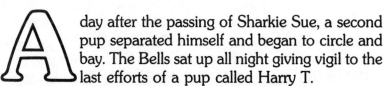day after the passing of Sharkie Sue, a second pup separated himself and began to circle and bay. The Bells sat up all night giving vigil to the last efforts of a pup called Harry T.

"Latonya," Oren asked, "do you know who Harry T. was going to be?"

"Harry T.," Latonya supplied, "was promised to the officers of the thirteenth precinct of the Detroit police department. Brenda has a night song made up for Harry T."

Brenda played the melody on her song flute a few times, then she handed the little flute to Granddaddy. No wind was left in his lungs to blow his silver horn, but Bill Bell made the song flute cry softly behind Brenda's sweet voice.

Harry T. Oh, Harry T.
was going to be
the greatest dog cop in Detroit historeeeeeeee
Harry T. Oh, Harry T.
doing his dog duties faith-ful-leeeeeeee
Harry T. Oh, Harry T.
sing along, all
We waaanna know
We waaannna know
where do angel puppies go?

By size, the puppies waited their turn for the solo death
dance. The mother dog and the old cat watched in dazed
resignation. Mama came home each night fearfully. Brenda
and Latonya lived in a fever of hope for the survivors.
Granddaddy stayed shocked sober, stirring the soup pot in
the kitchen, washing the dishes, polishing all surface space.
Latonya had never missed a day of school in her life, but
now she did. By the end of the week, it seemed reasonable
to turn the problem over to Granddaddy, although the family had never turned one over to him before. Not ever.

"What do you think we should do, Granddaddy?"
Latonya looked up at him from the floor where she was
stroking Buttercup.

Oren and Brenda also looked to Granddaddy, wondering
how the experiment would work out.

"Only one thing left to do." Bill Bell came to his feet so
fast, Skid fell to the floor. "First of all, Brenda, what do you
call the three little pups left in the basket?"

"The puppies are Glinda Good, Benjamin Bill, and the
biggest pup is call Tuffcity."

"Fine names, Brenda." Bill exhaled smoke thoughtfully and continued. "The answer to the problem simples down to this, we call in a veterinarian."

"Aunt Grace has a lady veterinarian," Latonya said.

"Not a vet who attends to that airhead, Fritz," Granddaddy said. "Desperate situations require specialists. We need a black, male veterinarian who knows all of the latest dog cures. Find one, Latonya."

"Granddaddy, a vet like that would cost a hundred dollars, if we could find one."

"Let Ms. Pugh find him," Granddaddy said. "And when she finds our man, Latonya, let me warn you, no poor-mouthing or begging. Understand? Glinda Good, Benjamin Bill, and Tuffcity deserve the vet's best shot. A hundred dollars should do it."

Granddaddy pulled his silver horn from under the sofa, opened the case, reached down into the bell of the horn and took out a roll of bills. He counted ten tens into Latonya's hand.

"If your mother knew I had all this money, she'd pay bills with it," he warned them gruffly.

Oren wondered why his sisters didn't look more surprised at Granddaddy having all that money. If he didn't know about the money, then they didn't know. Latonya expected there to be an honest or ghostly explanation to things she didn't know. Oren knew that most things had either a real or dishonest answer to them.

Ms. Pugh feared that Buttercup and her babies might infect other, less sick, dogs if they were taken to a veterinary clinic, so she convinced a doctor who taught dog medicine at Michigan State University to make a house call. She did this convincing by phone, without seeing the veterinarian in person. She said he sounded like a man, but she couldn't recognize the color of his complexion by his voice. He specialized in contagious animal infections. It was the best she could do.

On the day of the house call, Latonya cleaned the house twice and put some new meat in the soup pot. Michigan State University was a distance outside Detroit, and the vet might be hungry. Ms. Pugh told them the name of the vet was Jack Daniels, and Granddaddy said they could trust the man by the sound of his name. When the vet finally came in the front door, he appeared to meet all of Granddaddy's specifications. The way Latonya and Mama looked at Daniels, Oren knew he must be handsome by girl standards; however, there was something about this vet that Oren didn't like.

Dr. Daniels listened to Latonya relate the terrible fate that had befallen the puppies. He nodded his head wisely and looked his little patients over. When the vet explained what he thought the problem was, his voice sounded like he was giving a weather forecast. He explained that the mother dog was passing on some form of street distemper to her children, an illness common to dogs of her kind. It took him a minute to tell them why the puppies were dying, another five to instruct them what to do about it. Ms. Pugh took more time and got more worked up over describing a problem in long division. Still, Oren admitted, the vet was probably giving them his best shot. How could Jack Daniels know that poor Buttercup had gotten the disease from the house, not the street; just like Spiro and his family had gotten their killer disease from the house?

Dr. Daniels outlined his plan. "Take the pups away from the mother dog immediately. Buttercup's milk is contaminated. Formula and antibiotics must be administered to the pups every four hours around the clock."

"Will the puppies live?" Latonya said.

"I would be surprised if any of the pups survived." He continued writing and did not look up. Finished with the pups, Dr. Daniels turned his attention to Skid, sitting on top of the refrigerator.

"Has that cat always been cross-eyed?" Daniels demanded.

Brenda picked up on Oren's feelings concerning Jack Daniels, and gave the vet her best stupid-dinosaur look. She reserved such looks for new enemies. Her dinosaur expression often put off unwanted visitors from coming back.

Latonya, always the polite one, explained, "Skid's eyes are cockeyed, not cross-eyed. Skid has other scars from alley battles, but he is a strong old cat and throws off injuries without human help."

The tall, dark, handsome vet reached easily up to the top of the refrigerator and proceeded to rudely touch Skid's lumps. Skid held still for it, seeming to know the man's hands held some authority to probe him.

"This cat is too old for surgery. Keep him comfortable, and he may last the winter out."

Mama gasped, because Aunt Grace had warned her that Skid's lumps were contagious. "Is it safe for the children to handle Skid?"

"Children do not catch cancer from touching cats, dear

lady," Daniels assured Mama with an uppity air but warm-
ing smile.

With insight into more upcoming doom, Oren observed
Jack Daniels noticing how beautiful his mother was. Most
men noticed this, but Mama never held still for it. Mama
had many burdens to carry, and the last thing she needed
was a boyfriend.

Latonya inquired of Dr. Daniels how many dollars did
they owe him for his advice and medicine. Without thinking
on it, he charged them fifty dollars, saying that he would be
back the following week. Oren knew for sure that the next
visit would kill Granddaddy's hundred bucks. Mama accompanied the veterinarian to the front door. Oren went behind
and listened. Mama sounded like she was putting Jack Daniels off, but she was doing it in a very friendly way.

Latonya took charge of Glinda Good. Benjamin Bill became Brenda's responsibility. Ms. Pugh adopted Buttercup.
Latonya assigned Tuffcity to Oren and Granddaddy. Now
each morning before Oren went to school, he helped
Latonya make up the puppy formula for the day. Combin-
ing Karo syrup and skim milk, they poured the mixture into
doll-sized sterile bottles. Oren placed his pup firmly in his
lap, rolled the round little body over on its back; then he
forced the nipple of the bottle into the pup's mouth. When
the bottle was empty, Oren dropped medicine with a drop-
per down the tiny throat. Finally he turned the pup over to
Skid, who licked Tuffcity from nose to tail.

Granddaddy and Skid were responsible for puppy care
while Oren and his sisters were in school. Oren felt the
sorriest for Latonya, who was too worried and sad to con-

centrate on her schoolwork or keep Fred in line. Fred was
no help. Buddies were supposed to help and comfort their
appointed buddies. That was the system. Fred was taking a
lot of days off from school, and when he did show up, he
didn't even bother asking Latonya how the puppies were
doing. Blue and Whitey were into their own thing, which
was computers. Dink stayed upstairs so he wouldn't catch a
disease. Only Wesley Wrigley Fry came home with them
each day after school and helped out with the puppies until
her mama picked her up. Wesley cried sometimes and got
in the way, but her heart was in the right place.

Tuffcity grew stronger each day. But, alas, before two
weeks had passed, Glinda Good and Benjamin Bill circled
and bayed their sorrow at leaving; still they had to go.

"Granddaddy," Brenda pleaded, "how can heaven be big
enough to hold all of the puppies and kittens who die?"

"I am surprised at you, Brenda Bell," Granddaddy said.
"You, a number genius, questioning the size of a 'no limit'
place like heaven. Heaven is so big that it even has room
for rabbits. You rescued those little dogs from a lonely
death, all forsaken underneath the house next door. Every
pup needs a loving hand to hold its paw when its time
comes to cross over. You were there. You held fast to the
end. God knows the name of Glinda Good and Benjamin
Bill because you gave them a name. Our wise vet, Jack
Daniels, claims that Tuffcity is going to make it. You girls
enjoy our miracle pup. Oren Bell and myself need some
relief from him. He does look cute, sleeping under the soup
beside Skid. I hope, before long, Skid takes him outside
and teaches him how to do his business where it belongs, in
the weeds by the house next door."

"Listen, Oren," Latonya said, "this pup needs shots, dog food, a license, obedience school. Granddaddy's money has preserved him, and now it is up to you and me to get out and earn the money to provide dog essentials."

"Latonya," Oren brought up a new concern, "Mama is going to the movies with Dr. Daniels on Saturday night. I heard her say yes to him at the end of his last visit. She had to force him to take Granddaddy's last fifty bucks. Jack didn't want our money. What do you make of that?"

"Don't worry. Nothing will come of it. Mama is human enough to be tempted by a handsome man who offers a free movie, but Mama sees and Mama knows. She will judge Jack Daniels to be unfit."

The puppy crisis over, Granddaddy returned to his old disappearing tricks.

"Oren," Latonya said, "I'm holding back on practicing Sousa in hope of keeping Granddaddy at home, but he still leaves. Where do you think he goes? Do you think he has a job and he's too proud to tell us?"

"Maybe," Oren lied. He knew that Bill Bell didn't believe in either welfare or work. On occasion Bill had sold his blood to buy cigs and Red Rose wine, but Oren believed he had used up all of his extra blood.

"Well, here's a piece of good news. My buddy, Fred, is on his way over."

"Some nerve. You want me to get rid of him for you?"

"Oren, you are so small-minded. Indians have been discriminated against for hundreds of years, and it's the fault of people like you. If I can help Fred catch up in school, then it will make up for some of the injury that was done to Fred's people."

When Fred showed up, he aimed his full charm at Latonya. "Girl, I hear you've been busy taking care of sick dogs. I see you've got one left that didn't croak."

"Nice of you to take an interest, Fred. Ms. Pugh is keeping Buttercup, and this little guy is Tuffcity."

"Real bad, Latonya. Could we pick up on my school work? I don't have all night."

"Sure, Fred. Push Brenda's ship pictures off the dining room table and let's get started."

When Fred was ready to leave, Oren offered to walk him to the corner.

"Hey man, you brave enough to walk right past the house next door?"

"Fred, tell me straight. Does Granddaddy hang out in there?"

"Don't jive me, Oren. You know he does."

"I mean, is he staying there now? It's going down to zero degrees tonight with the windchill factor. Granddaddy is frail as a rail."

"Look at the house, Oren. There's smoke coming out the chimney. Some things are turned on in the house."

"Is Granddaddy making money off the house?"

"Not like me. No money to speak about."

"But some money?"

"I guess it's safe to tell you. My boss has to keep records, but not for too long. You get what I mean? Bill sits in the parlor and starts a little fire in the fireplace to keep him warm while he drinks his bottle of wine. He doesn't get much money for burning the house trash but enough for his booze and cigs. That's all he needs. Bill got behind in his trash burning during the puppy crisis. Now the house demands that he catch up. See you around, Oren."

It's a terrible loneliness not to like an old friend. There was smoke coming out of the chimney. Oren's attention shifted to movement in his own driveway. Jack Daniels's Mustang was pulling in like it belonged there. The year had been cursed to the worse, and he knew who was to blame. The house was menacing his family and separating him from his friends.

Chapter 9

o　o　o

After Thanksgiving, Brenda got sick. It was never a coughing, burning up, all-out emergency when Brenda got sick. Brenda enjoyed her little sicknesses and it was no trick for her to make up work in school. It might not be safe to leave Brenda with Granddaddy, but what else could they do?

On this day, Oren was glad that Latonya had him all to herself for the walk home from school. He had serious family problems to talk over with her.

"Latonya, what do you think about the way that Jack Daniels is coming around and taking over? He could be trying to move in like Aunt Grace's husbands try to do."

"Maybe it's time Mama had a boyfriend."

"But him?"

"Face it, Oren. Jack Daniels is rich, handsome, and smart."

Looks, money, and brains seemed to have swayed Latonya's and Mama's judgment. Oren moved on to the next problem.

"Mama says there are rumors and talk that the downtown J. L. Hudson Company Store, where she works, will be closed down. Soon. This year."

"How you worry on, Oren. That disaster will never come about. The downtown J. L. Hudson Company Store is the biggest department store in the world. It is the one and only store where the real Santa Claus feels comfortable after the Thanksgiving Day Parade."

Poor Latonya. She believed in Santa Claus. She trusted that he hadn't cheated on the ceremony. When they came in the front door, they found Granddaddy and Brenda watching television. The two of them seemed to be in a trance over the action on the screen.

"Come in. Sit down. Be quiet," Brenda directed them. "And don't sit on Spiro or step on the puppy. This story is called *A Night to Remember,* and it is about the biggest, saddest ship-sinking ever."

Oren sat down with them to watch. Mama was home, and Latonya joined her in the kitchen. He could see why Brenda and Granddaddy liked the movie. It was all about rich people who lived in the days of Spiro Spill. There must have been a thousand of them or so. They were all having a party on a floating palace. The palace was going to sink. It was clear enough that it had to sink, but none of the people believed it. Why did people refuse to believe that the worst was bound to happen? The huge, glittering ship was as

cursed and as doomed as the house next door. After the
ship and the partying people had gone down to the bottom
of the sea, like Oren knew they would, Latonya called dinner. She was serving ribs and mashed potatoes, and for
once they didn't have to share with Aunt Grace or Jack
Daniels.

Mama and Latonya were so into their girl talk that they
didn't eat much. Brenda chattered on about the *Titanic,*
and how she was going to draw it for the rest of her life.
Granddaddy was never able to keep food in his stomach, so
he smoked a cig and did what Mama called his philosophizing. Tonight there was plenty of food for Oren Bell, so
he ate and listened.

"Did you notice how that *Titanic* band kept playing while
the ship went down?" Granddaddy let his words and smoke
roll out like gassy pearls. "Many brave horns are asleeeep in
the deeeep."

"Hurry up and finish your eating and talking," Brenda
urged them. "I need the dining room table for my first *Titanic* picture."

"Jack has asked me to accompany him to a performance
of the Detroit Symphony on Saturday night," Mama said.

"Oh, Mama," Latonya gushed. "What will you wear?"

"It just so happens that I put a gorgeous dress on
layaway, and matching shoes too. Latonya, Jack will come
in from Lansing on Friday night and sleep over. I trust that
we can make him comfortable."

His worst fear was happening. "Where will he sleep?"
Oren asked his mama. He knew this question was bound to
calm her down. Latonya could never scrub the Red Rose
fumes out of Granddaddy's room, and Brenda's bed-wet-

ting had whiffed the charm right out of the purple bedroom.

"I think the living room is our best bet," Latonya said.
"We could build a fire in the fireplace, and that would make
it homey. Jack could sleep on the sofa, and Oren could
sleep in the chair."

"That arrangement would give Oren and Jack an opportunity to get acquainted," Mama said.

Jack Daniels was going to sleep on his sofa? Oren liked
the idea. Jack's body would be instantly sucked in and
stabbed to death. If Jack's body did escape death, the pain
would keep him from coming back in a hurry.

"Mama"—he changed the subject—"if the J. L. Hudson
Company closes down after Christmas like the rumors
claim, then where will all the shoppers and the workers
go?"

"The shoppers will shop at suburban malls, and the workers with most seniority will go to Hudson's mall stores."

She didn't say where Santa Claus was going. Most likely
to the malls, although Oren knew that Santa Claus was
nincompoopery.

The tidings of Jack Daniels's visit set Latonya off on an
all-out effort to sterilize and decorate. The cleaning action
started the following day after school.

"Brenda, get your ship pictures off the living room wall.
There are nasty tape spots everywhere I look. Oren and
Blue, you guys hunt up the white paint in the basement,
and start painting the ceiling and the bricks around the
fireplace. I'll get right on washing the curtains."

"Latonya, we only have one day after today." Oren tried to calm her down.

"A point well made, Oren. We will keep the bedroom doors closed at all times, and restrict Jack Daniels to the living room and kitchen. That still gives us plenty to do. Get moving. Granddaddy, do you think you could get Tuffcity trained to do his business outdoors by Friday?"

"No, Latonya, I don't. Jack Daniels has seen puppy poop before."

"I refuse to take my pictures down for old Jack Daniels." Brenda lay on her stomach creating a large and colorful seascape of the sinking of the *Titanic*. "Latonya, Granddaddy is drawing all of the drowning people and I have to draw portholes."

"Granddaddy is doing a fine job on drowning people"— Latonya gave that round to Granddaddy—"but both of you get to your jobs."

Jack Daniels moved in about seven o'clock Friday evening. He intended staying on until Sunday evening. He was wearing faded old jeans, bringing along his dress-up clothes in a neat hanger bag. Without waiting for direction from Latonya, he marched into the purple bedroom. Even worse, he opened the closet door and moved aside the hidden living room junk. He pushed and shoved to make space for his own belongings. Then he went into the kitchen and bothered Mama and Latonya while they were trying to get dinner ready. After dinner, he put papers on the kitchen table and started to bother the cat.

"Oren, hold Skid for me, while I remove his matted hair." Oren decided to go along with the hair mat operation.

Skid might take Jack Daniels's attention away from the rest of the family. Brenda was busy putting her sinking-ship pictures back up on the living room wall. Latonya was forgetting to keep her voice down in front of Mama's friend. It was early in the evening, but Granddaddy's face was settling into his pleasant Red Rose smile. Mama didn't show it, but Oren knew she was humiliated by the way they were all carrying on.

It was difficult to see where the hard mats of hair left off and the cat skin began. How could he be sure that Jack Daniels knew what he was doing?

"Dr. Daniels," Oren gave him full respect, "I'm afraid you're hurting Skid. Besides that, Latonya doesn't allow cats on the kitchen table."

"Seems to me," Jack said, "there are others around here doing what Latonya tells them not to do. Skid needs to be groomed. Keep holding, Oren."

Oren continued holding. By Sunday night, Jack would be gone. The man was supplying them with free dog food and cat food, plus pup vitamins and Senior Purr Vitapets. Still, Daniels had only been in the Bell house for a few hours and Oren was sick of the sight of him.

Saturday morning, Jack went jogging. He didn't wear a coat or jacket, because he believed if he ran fast enough the cold wouldn't get him. When Jack returned, they all sat down to breakfast, with the exception of Granddaddy, who was hung over from the night before, and never ate breakfast.

"About that house next door," Jack started off. "It would be a fine house for a family to restore and live in. It has character and good lines."

Latonya gasped and Brenda giggled. If Jack Daniels had his way, he would marry Mama and move them all into the house next door.

"Dr. Daniels," Oren tried to set Jack straight. "It's complete nincompoopery, but the house next door happens to be haunted and vicious. It gets people. Even ghosts are smart enough to stay away from it."

"All true," Latonya backed him up. "We would be having bad luck right now, if we hadn't given that house a reverse curse on the first day of school."

Jack thought this over while he ate his eggs.

Latonya and Brenda loved seeing Mama dressed up for the symphony concert. Oren had never seen Mama all glowing in a long silver dress. Mama was laughing like she didn't have a serious thought in her head. Oren wondered if it was good for her to be so happy. Jack Daniels had cleaned himself up to handsome, but he used the bathroom a long time in doing it. The sight of Mama's beauty seemed to quiet the man's mouth down. Still, he was no Prince Charming. After Mama and Jack were gone, Granddaddy sobered up, and the four of them spent the evening drawing drowning people.

When Mama and Jack came home from the concert, Oren woke up. He listened to them talking in the kitchen. When they were quiet, he was afraid they were kissing. He hoped not. They probably were. Maybe he should go out to the kitchen. Finally Jack came in and lay himself down on the sofa. The sofa didn't seem to give him any trouble. Oren decided to let Jack know that he was awake. It was time to straighten out the poor guy's thinking. Jack believed Mama to be a beautiful lady who went around laughing in a long party dress. The bare bones truth was that Mama wore a uniform at the J. L. Hudson Company, old jeans around the house, and a very ordinary dress on Sundays. Also, it was more natural for her to be troubled than to smile and laugh like a princess. He thought his words over carefully, because he didn't want Daniels to think Mama wasn't elegant enough for symphony concerts.

"You know, Dr. Daniels, our mama has turned down many dress-up jobs in office buildings, because the pay was too low. Aunt Grace cannot pay her share of the bills. Mama needs to be a serious worker at all times." His words sounded hard to his ear, so he softened some. "Brenda gets sick a lot. Our family has decided outside activities have to wait until Brenda grows up. Nothing against you, Jack, but Mama has no time for boyfriends."

"That is very interesting, Oren," Jack commented. "I appreciate hearing it."

Feeling confident that he had now taken care of the problem, Oren could curl up in the chair and go to sleep.

By morning, Jack had forgotten their little talk. He called Mama "honey." He called her by her name, Sarah. He called her "Sarah honey."

"Sarah, honey, does Grandfather Bell receive social security benefits?"

Off on a Sunday morning wine hunt, Granddaddy was mercifully spared listening to Jack's insults.

"No," Mama sighed. "Grandfather Bell isn't old enough yet for social security benefits."

"How old is he?" Jack persisted.

"Fifty-nine years," Mama said.

Mama looked guilty because Aunt Grace had been harping on her to kick Granddaddy out, or at least to find a way to turn his stay into a welfare check.

"Does your father-in-law work?"

"I don't think he works," Mama apologized.

Latonya and Brenda watched with worried eyes, waiting for their brother to defend Granddaddy.

"Where does he get his booze money? Why doesn't he work?" Jack kept at Mama.

"My father-in-law, Bill Bell, played a trumpet by trade, but his wind ran out." Mama explained it simple enough so even Jack ought to understand.

"Seems to me Bill could find some kind of work; taxi driver, dishwasher, night watchman. I did jobs like that when I was in college, and I'd do them again. For God's sake, Sarah, you clean out toilets."

Oren knew he had better say or do something quick, but what?

Jack seemed to pick up on how his words were wounding Mama, so he lightened up and tried to make amends.

"How about us all going out to dinner somewhere? We could try a foreign country, like Canada. How about it?"

Oren said, "No way." Mama and the girls liked the idea. Jack sure knew ways to tempt ladies. After they were gone, Oren played with the puppy and drew a few drowning people. He kept his eye on the front door, praying Granddaddy would get home before they came back, so he could whip him out of sight. As usual, the Lord screwed up on the timing.

Jack, Mama, and the girls came back in high spirits. They

brought Oren a little bag of food. People in Canada must eat Chinese. Mama, smiling again, went to the kitchen to make coffee and hot chocolate. Jack Daniels, always thinking up ways to push himself into the family, settled his long body down on the floor between Brenda and Latonya. He said he wanted to draw some drowning people. Lucky the *Titanic* needed so many. Brenda didn't like Jack's drowning people, so she put him on smokestacks. About this time, Granddaddy made his entrance. Smiling his Red Rose smile, Bill staggered through the door. He tottered a moment, giving Jack and the girls time to move quick. When he fell, he fell headlong on top of the *Titanic* picture, clipping the pup on his crash down. Tuffcity yipped so loud that Aunt Grace started banging on the ceiling. Brenda howled along with the pup. All the noise brought Granddaddy around. He sat up and gave them all a puzzled look. Having inherited Latonya's weak stomach, Bill then threw up Red Rose wine all over the *Titanic.* He bloodied the drowning people, the waves, the portholes, the smokestacks, the icebergs; then he fell facedown again on the ruins and broke Brenda's best Crayolas. For a long moment, they all stared at the sorry sight. Before Oren could move to action, Jack Daniels picked Granddaddy up like he was a baby and carried him off to bed. Mama held Brenda. Latonya cleaned up the mess. There was nothing left for Oren to do. Jack Daniels had carried out the family job that rightfully belonged to him. When Granddaddy's snores settled down to a normal Red Rose frequency, Jack started up on Mama again.

"Sarah, you do that man no service," he insisted, like it was some business of his.

Mama kept on rocking Brenda and didn't look at Jack. This time Jack took no notice of Mama's misery.

"Your father-in-law belongs in a hospital."

Oren racked his brain for a good word to put in for his grandfather. He found one.

"My Granddaddy fought in the big war. That's more than you can say, Jack Daniels."

This information got Jack all excited. "You hit on the solution, Oren. If your grandfather fought in a war, he is entitled to veterans' benefits. The Veterans Hospital in Allen Park might take him." Jack Daniels kissed Mama in front of her own children and was gone. Oren knew they hadn't seen the last of him.

"Mama," Oren pleaded, "don't let Jack send Grand-daddy away."

"I support Oren one hundred percent on this issue," Latonya said. "Granddaddy sots his brain and smokes the air out of his lungs, but he is our responsibility."

"Responsibility," Brenda voted with them, rolling out a vast amount of paper across the living room floor. Oren suspected she was embarking on a new *Titanic.*

Still under the influence of Jack's kissing, Mama reasoned on the other side. "Jack says he sees blood coming out of Bill's coughing. While we believe it to be all red wine, it should be checked by a doctor. We don't have the money for a checkup. If Jack finds a way to get him into a hospital, your grandfather might be made whole again."

"Once a hospital gets hold of Granddaddy, they will never let him go," Brenda advised, sketching in the first iceberg.

Brenda was right. A hopeless feeling gripped Oren. He

was the one who had handed Jack Daniels the idea—the idea on how to get rid of Granddaddy.

After the girls were bedded down for the night, Oren checked on Bill's breathing. He was still doing it. Back to the sofa, Oren curled himself around the sprung springs. What terrible thing was going to happen next? Skid crawled in beside him. Oren held the purring old cat close to his chest. The house knew how to grab his ideas and use them to get rid of the people he loved.

Chapter 10

o   o   o

I t was all arranged. Two o'clock on the afternoon of
Christmas eve, Jack Daniels showed up. When Jack
left, Granddaddy would be going with him. Mama
explained to Oren and his sisters that Granddaddy
had to be in the hospital by the night of Christmas eve. If
Jack didn't sign Granddaddy in when a bed opened up,
some other sick veteran would get his bed. Granddaddy
was quiet about his having to go to a hospital. He didn't
object to it. Bill had never been much for Christmas anyway. He always said he believed in receiving gifts but not in
giving any. The week before, the family had put up the tree.
Since that time, Granddaddy spent his hours gazing at the
tree. In years past, Mama had bought trimmings for the tree
at the after-Christmas sales at the J. L. Hudson Company.

This year the Bell tree was fully trimmed. Latonya and Brenda strung popcorn on the branches. The tree stood in the tree corner where Brenda claimed Spiro had set up the Spill tree. Brenda knew stuff like that. Mama had taken the day off from her job. It was the J. L. Hudson Company's biggest day of the year, but it was Granddaddy's going-away day, and Mama knew she was needed at home. The Bells expected to sit down together to a turkey dinner, and then open gifts. Jack refused Aunt Grace and her group permission to come down and eat, but he granted himself permission to stay.

Granddaddy started talking at the table, his first words in a week.

"Listen, Jack, do you think our puppy is hyper? I'd hate to see the little critter turn out foolish, like Fritz Bell."

"Normal puppy high spirits," Jack assured him.

"I admire the shape of our tree, but let's leave off those blinking lights next year. Drives a fellow crazy to sit around all day, watching and waiting for the nervous things to blink on and off. Skid objects to them too. The turkey smells good. You sure are a good cook, Latonya—like your grandmother, Hazel Bell."

"Granddaddy," Latonya corrected, "my grandmother is Betty Bell. Hazel Bell was a different wife to you. Why do you always make that blunder?"

"Trying to forget Betty Bell," he retorted, with some of his old mean spirit.

The gift unwrapping after dinner moved right along. Granddaddy reminded them that they didn't have time to waste. He opened Latonya's gift first to make up for not liking her grandmother, Betty Bell.

"Latonya, I've watched you making these slippers for the past year, all the time wondering whose feet they were meant to fit. Should have given me a clue when you kept holding them up to my feet."

Jack gifted Granddaddy with a ten-inch television set, so he wouldn't miss his reruns and game shows while he was in the hospital. Mama presented him with a new bathrobe with a velvet collar. Oren's gift was a framed picture of the pup and cat. Jack had taken the picture with his camera and blown it up, but Oren had made the frame in school. Granddaddy admired the picture. Brenda gave him a new *Titanic* picture, along with her broken Crayolas, which she had cleaned up. Granddaddy requested that each one of them draw one drowning person on the bottom of his picture. He wanted to remember how each of them drew. He said he liked his gifts.

It was time for Granddaddy to go. He dragged his silver horn case from beneath the sofa. For one uneasy minute Oren feared that his grandfather was going to present him with the silver horn. Bill Bell cradled the horn case in his arms and followed Jack out the door without looking back. His departure hung heavy for a long moment.

"I failed." Mama sighed, not making it clear what it was she had failed at.

Oren came by her side and took her hand. "You can't do everything, Mama."

The girls came close, and the four of them sat together, watching the tree lights blink on and off. Mama sighed again and started unburdening herself to them.

"The downtown J. L. Hudson Company Store is closing

next month and I am afraid that I don't have the seniority to be placed in a suburban mall."

"No, Mama," Latonya objected. "The J. L. Hudson Company will stand forever in downtown Detroit on Woodward Avenue."

When Latonya talked about the J. L. Hudson Company, a wild patriotic gleam lit up her face. She was like Ms. Pugh that way. Well, why not? A person had to depend on something. The reason that Latonya still felt hopeful was because she didn't know Oren had opened his eye during the ceremony.

Mama didn't answer Latonya, because Mama knew that the poor girl was a positive thinker. Positive thinkers were nice to have around, but a person couldn't trust their opinions.

Suddenly, bright-beam lights came through the window and lit up the whole room. Sirens shattered the silent night and set the pup and cat on edge. The Bells ran to the window.

"I expect another terrible tragedy has happened in the house next door," Oren said.

"Bet they found a new body." Brenda leaned her cheek against the window.

His Granddaddy was safe in the old soldiers' hospital, Oren reminded himself. If the cops found a body, it wouldn't be him.

They all jumped at the loud thump on the door.

"It's only Blue," Brenda assured them.

Oren was embarrassed at not recognizing his friend's secret thump, but his heart pounding in his head blocked out his sense of the ordinary. Mama had to tell him to let Blue in.

"This time it's a kid," Blue informed them with an air of importance. "My brother is next door with the other cops from the Thirteenth. I heard him say that the new body is a kid."

"Basil Brown, what are you talking about?" Mama demanded. She swept a glance around the room to make sure her children were all accounted for and present.

"He's talking about the new body in the house next door being a kid, Mama," Brenda said.

"Right," Blue expanded as a bearer of bad news. "The house next door's most recent victim is a kid. I don't know who the body belongs to, but the police called Ms. Pugh. I gotta go. My mother says I am not allowed out after dark until I am thirty-five years old. Now that the house is out to get kids, we all need to be more careful."

The body couldn't be Fred, Oren told himself. Bodies turned out to be strangers, not friends. The house was Fred's crib. Even the house next door wouldn't be that cruel. Fred always said he had the house under control.

Mama rang up Aunt Grace on the phone. Dink and Dede were safe in bed with her, and Fritz Bell was doing his duty by barking in the backyard. Aunt Grace didn't feel like venturing downstairs or talking on the phone. She wanted to get back to putting her head under the covers. Latonya and Brenda urged Mama to call Jack. Mama liked that idea, so she followed their advice. Jack wanted to return to Detroit immediately, and protect them from the house next door. Mama said, "No way, Jack. You have responsibilities in Lansing. I won't hear of you coming back tonight." Alerting and worrying Jack to the danger seemed to steady and satisfy Mama's nerves. Now she was ready to do the sensible thing. She told Oren he was the man of the house. She told Latonya to put Brenda to bed, and then she went to bed herself.

Oren unplugged the Christmas tree, checked the locks on both doors, then lay down on the sofa with his clothes on. Skid purred in beside him. The cat and him were a comfort to each other. The pup was a bother, chewing on his foot and making puppy growls. Oren and Skid looked at the police lights playing on the ceiling. Oren thought about Jack Daniels.

It was time that he gave serious thought to Jack. Jack was big and strong and he knew useful information. Jack loved Mama and he tolerated Latonya and Brenda. Oren had to allow, Jack tried. Most people didn't do that. Another good thing about Jack, he wasn't apt to take off like their real daddy had done. Jack was the kind who stuck to a family like cement. He sort of wished that Jack had come back. Oren turned his attention to Latonya and Brenda hassling each other in the purple bedroom. First Brenda would take off on her night song, then Latonya would hush her down. Oren listened better, hoping Brenda's night song would be about Granddaddy's leaving. It wasn't. Brenda was singing one of her nonsense songs. Why was Brenda singing a nonsense song when there was real sorrow to sing about?

him and thee
you and me

114

her and he
I and she

Brenda was nearly as good at pronouns as she was numbers.

"You shut up, Brenda Bell, before I put a shoe in your
mouth," Latonya shouted.

"I'm singing my night song." Brenda went to a higher
pitch, and Oren knew that Brenda was singing straight into
Latonya's eardrum.

him and thee
you and me
will you jump into the sea
her and he
I and she
or
would you rather sink with me

For one chorus her song became muffled, but then it rose
high and clear, filling the flat with little-girl screams.

will you jump into the sea
quietly, smoothly, oozily
will you slip into the sea
or
would you rather sink with me
sink with me
sink with me
to the bottom of the sea
you and me

he and she
them and thee
all of we
to the bottom of the sea

Oren heard Mama stomping to Latonya's rescue. Jack
had warned them that Brenda was drawing too many
drowning people for an eight-year-old girl. Latonya had explained to Jack that Brenda needed to finish Granddaddy's
picture before he left for the hospital. The family was accus-
tomed to Brenda's weirdness and sassiness and didn't mind
it. The downstairs flat on Fourth Street quieted down.
Mama was staying the night in the purple bedroom with the
girls and Spiro Spill.

Chapter 11

o   o   o

When Ms. Pugh told them that the body in the house next door belonged to Fred Lightfoot, Latonya came down with a case of the self-put-downs. The girl didn't know how to put her brain on neutral the way Oren did. Latonya's high demands on herself often caused her to have an upset stomach, but this time she was in more serious trouble. Jack Daniels held back on giving his thoughts on the problem, and Oren gave him credit for it. Latonya's main symptom was her mouth. It ran on without stopping. She blamed herself for Fred's murder. She might have blamed her twin brother if she knew that he had opened his eyes during the ceremony, but Oren was sure that knowing wouldn't help her. Latonya had taken on the woes of the world. His poor headsick sister confessed to Oren how the shock of Fred's killing had scrambled her wits beyond repair.

"Admit it. Don't spare me, Oren," she wailed. "Ms. Pugh assigned me to be Fred's buddy. I was the one responsible for the boy's safety."

"Sometimes you did a good job," Oren assured her. "Remember back in September at the zoo trip? When Fred jumped into the walrus pool, you jumped in after him and stayed till help came. Remember in October, at the art museum trip? When Fred tried to escape out the window of the men's room, you held fast to his legs while strange men cursed you. You held fast, Latonya."

"I fell down when the big challenge came along."

"Latonya, Fred wasn't on any class trip when the house got him. You are off the hook on that one, girl. Fred was doing dirty business inside the house. His own foster mama couldn't keep him out of the house. Let up on yourself, Latonya."

"It was my responsibility, Oren. Fred's trusting foster mama believed all the boy's lies. He ran through foster mamas so fast, not one of them got to know him like I did. Fred lacked a proper upbringing. I should have brought him up. Fred consorted with evil people all up and down Third and Cass. He slept inside the house next door. I knew it, but I didn't put a stop to it. If I had tracked Fred down for all of the band practices, he might have learned to blow well enough to deserve Granddaddy's silver horn, and the pride of it would have straightened him out. Fred held such promise, and I failed to make him shine."

When Latonya slowed down on taking blame for Fred's murder, she started blaming herself for long-past disasters.

"You know, Oren, I believe it was my fault that our daddy left us. More than likely, in good time, I will drive off Jack Daniels. Daddy didn't mind you and Brenda all that much, Oren. It was me who set him on edge. I am like my grandmother, Betty Bell."

Neither Latonya nor Oren had ever seen Betty Bell, but Granddaddy had spoken of her often. Betty Bell scolded angels when humans refused to sit still for it. Betty Bell worked for a mean collection agency, so she could earn a good paycheck by going after people she didn't know. Betty Bell wore long pants because she was bowlegged.

"I hope I die before I ruin Mama's chances with Jack," Latonya ran on. "I bet we have seen the last of that wonderful, rich animal doctor."

"Jack fears and respects you, Latonya. He called a while ago to say snow and sleet are blocking all roads out of Lansing, but he's coming through anyway. Betty Bell, herself in person, couldn't back that guy off."

It disturbed Oren to see how Brenda behaved during Latonya's time of trial. His smallest sister's bed-wetting became a nightly habit. Brenda started doing nothing in school. Her teacher couldn't teach the rest of the class with Brenda making a dinosaur face at her. The school suggested that Brenda stay home for a while. Mama was committed to seeing the J. L. Hudson Company through its final sale days. There was nothing to do but call on Aunt Grace for baby-sitting help. Aunt Grace didn't like dinosaur faces any better than Brenda's teacher did. When Mama came in the door tired, before she could get her coat off,

Brenda stretched out her arms to be rocked. Oren and Latonya couldn't satisfy her. Jack spent his date time solving Oren's long-division problems, listening to Latonya berate herself, and training the pup. When Aunt Grace complained about having to baby-sit Brenda, Jack blew his top. Jack had never been good at tolerating Aunt Grace.

"It won't hurt you to pitch in once in a while, Grace. Brenda needs a little loving care, now stretch to it."

Oren attempted to talk his little sister out of her spoiled performance.

"You hear me, Brenda? Straighten up. We don't need any of your dinosaur faces around here. January is a cold month for the people of Detroit. A maniac runs loose in our neighborhood because the cops drove him out of the house next door. Aunt Grace is having Dink and Dede bussed over to Jefferson School because she says Spiro Spill School is a sinking ship. The J. L. Hudson Company is also a sinking ship. Aunt Grace threatens to call the dog pound about Tuffcity's yapping. Old Skid has a new lump that Jack doesn't like the looks of. Latonya lets our soup steam away on its own. We need cheer around this place, so you just cheer up, Brenda Bell."

Declining Oren's invitation to brighten up the corner where she was, Brenda moped down into a deeper hole, with nobody invited inside except Spiro Spill.

Spiro Spill Elementary was for sure a sinking ship. Before Fred's murder, the dangers of the neighborhood had been known but ignored. Fires broke out. Ghosts haunted boarded-up houses. A drug dealer or a lady of the night came to a violent end. It was never a big deal. Then Fred fell, and there were cops guarding the school route. Police protection wasn't good enough. Teachers and students alike came down with school flu and stayed home.

Ms. Pugh smiled sadly at what was left of her once-bold class. "Latonya, Wesley, Oren, Blue, and White," she said, "you are my brave and faithful five."

She no longer had Kimberly Banks to give her a "why." Conrad Cord wasn't around to provoke her. Dink Bell had fled to Jefferson School and taken all of his mediums along with him.

"Dear friends," Ms. Pugh continued, "on Monday all S.S. students will be taken by bus to the school in the Jefferson project, there to complete the term under the direction of a new teacher."

Oren spoke up because he was no longer shy. "You told us that Jefferson School is an example of what is wrong with education."

"You told us," Blue added, "that Jefferson School is nothing but a steel shed."

"True," Ms. Pugh admitted, "but an inquiring mind can find wisdom and knowledge inside a steel shed."

"I won't find any," Blue promised.

Oren knew his mama would make him find some.

"Ms. Pugh," Wesley said, "my mother is sending me to a school in Grosse Pointe, where we live. I won't be able to have Oren for a buddy anymore." Wesley burst into tears and Oren let her cry. Some things needed to be cried over.

Latonya was given permission to come up with one of her screwy thoughts. "Our airy castle must not fall to the invaders," she said.

Ms. Pugh picked up on his sister's words like they were

jewels. "A splendid analogy, Latonya. S.S. is like a castle of the Renaissance period. Renaissance means awakening of learning. If our castle falls to the wrecker's ball, let us keep its beauty and spirit of learning in our hearts. Let us not return to the dark ages."

Ms. Pugh crossed the room. The five of them followed her. Together they looked out the bay windows down to the busy expressway below. Not one of them had ever ventured out onto the porch adjoining the windows. It was against school safety rules. Famous for defying school rules, Fred Lightfoot had chanced the porch many times. High unprotected places made Oren feel funny. Being on an airy castle kick, there was no telling what Ms. Pugh had in mind, but she motioned the class to return to their seats.

"Four precious days left to study and experience the school's different spaces. We are the only class in the school. We are the last to leave. We will move around. Friday's math test will be taken down in the cellar, the dungeon, the bowels of S. S. Elementary."

The class was pleased with her plan. The network of secret rooms in the cellar had never before been opened to students. It was a neat way to leave a school.

"Can we carve our long division on the walls?" Oren asked.

"No reason not to," Ms. Pugh said. "We must work precisely, so that some future culture will decode our numbers and know that we were correct."

"Let's pretend," Wesley suggested, "that we're hiding out from the Spanish Inquisition. If one of us here makes an error, the dummy will be stretched on a rack, his legs and arms pulled out of their sockets, a big sharp knife swinging closer and closer over his screaming body."

"Holy Jesus," Whitey prayed. He was still working at a third-grade level in math.

Latonya wanted to stay after school and work out the details of her airy-castle scheme with Ms. Pugh. While he waited for Latonya, Oren decided to go downstairs to pick up his Spiro Spill trumpet, which had been awarded to him to keep. Seeing Mr. Shell sitting alone in the band room, Oren paused at the doorway.

"Come in, old man," Mr. Shell said.

They sat together for a while, gazing at the musical squares framing the fireplace. The major and minor keys, notes and scales, were all painted in blue on white ceramic tiles. Mr. Shell finally took his attention away from the tiles and regarded the big picture of a man hanging on the wall directly over the fireplace.

"Really unusual having a picture of Johann Sebastian Bach on the wall of a city school like this. Wouldn't you agree, old man?"

"I never gave it much thought, Mr. Shell." Oren studied the picture for the first time. Would the man in the picture turn out to be as important as Spiro Spill? Johann S. Bach looked suspiciously like Fred Lightfoot.

"Got something on my mind, old man." Mr. Shell's fretting eyes shifted from Bach, to Oren, to his own shoe, then back to Bach.

"Feel free," Oren encouraged.

"I am the one who is responsible for Fred's death." Mr. Shell covered his face with his hands.

Was Mr. Shell the maniac? Aunt Grace said that many teachers were perverts, and kids should look out for them.

"I looked into the possibility of adopting Fred," Mr. Shell said. "Even though I am an unmarried man who doesn't like children all that much, it appeared to be a perfect match. How many orphans have the musical potential of a Fred Lightfoot? I knew that adopting Fred would impress Ms. Pugh. She admired me for thinking of it. The social service department checked me out. They suggested Fred and I try the relationship for a weekend. Oren, it was the longest weekend of my life, two really terrible days in a row. I was relieved when the little 'son of a gun' escaped out my bathroom window. Excuse the language, old man."

Mr. Shell had called Fred worse names than that, but Oren could see that the band teacher was trying to improve.

"The bottom line is this, Oren. I could have gritted in there and made myself accountable for that fine little musician. I held back. Holding back on a good impulse is more terrible than not having one in the first place. I refused to bond myself to Fred. Now he's dead. I deserve contempt from Ms. Pugh and everybody."

"It is not all your fault, Mr. Shell. My sister accepts full responsibility for Fred's passing. Ms. Pugh feels she failed Fred. I could be more to blame than all of you put together. At least you taught him that he could hit high C if he practiced."

"Thank you, old man. By the way, the music program is over, but keep in touch. Bring your old S.S. horn by my apartment and we'll blow a few bars of the London Bridge Overture together."

Oren stood by the bay window in the music room and

watched Mr. Shell go to his car. Mr. Shell kicked the tires of his old Thunderbird, got inside and drove off. Oren went upstairs to get Latonya. It wasn't safe for him to walk home without her. Some disaster might be ready to happen again from the house next door, and he didn't want to be alone. He was glad that Mr. Shell hadn't pressed him into confessing why it was him that was the most to blame for Fred's murder.

Chapter 12

o   o   o

The Bell twins walked home from school in step. Sometimes Oren was glad to talk to Latonya. She knew what he was thinking and that saved time.

"Aunt Grace doesn't understand," Oren began.

"Our little Brenda's high spirits," Latonya finished. "So pick up your feet, Oren, and let's get home and take back our little sister. Aunt Grace has been on the edge since she carpeted her whole flat in white shaggy."

"How does she keep it so white?" Oren wondered.

"When and if Uncle Penn shows up, he takes his shoes off or he don't come in," Latonya said. "Fritz Bell stays to his chain in the backyard. Dink and Dede keep to their throw rug in front of the television set. Aunt Grace has discipline going for her at all times."

"When we give Brenda to Aunt Grace, she acts like we tossed her a stink bomb," Oren stated a hard fact.

"Like we tossed her a stink bomb," Latonya repeated.

"Aunt Grace has trouble keeping our Brenda on a throw rug. No pups, no cats, no ghosts, no Crayolas allowed in her upstairs flat." Oren came to full attention. "Latonya, there's a cop car and a fire engine in front of our house." They started to run in step.

"They must be there for the house next door." Latonya kept full speed beside him.

It appeared to Oren that the trouble was at their place, but Aunt Grace was there caring for Brenda. Brenda had to be safe.

A small crowd hopped up and down in front of the Bell house, the temperature sending their breathing up in little puffs. Oren picked out Aunt Grace. She was shrilling a fireman with the particulars of the emergency. Brenda Bell had done something really awful, but Oren couldn't make out what it was. Brenda never played with matches. The house couldn't be on fire. The firemen were standing around making no attempt to ax down the front door. The hoses lay intact on the side of the fire truck. Oren and Latonya bounded up the steps and in the front door of their house. Blue's brother and Jack stood in the living room talking.

"We have to get her down before Sarah comes home," Jack insisted grimly. Seeing Oren and Latonya, he hugged Latonya and shook hands with Oren.

"Dear God, I'm glad to see you two. Brenda is sitting on top of the roof with the pup and the cat. We don't know how they got up there, or how we are going to get them down. The heavy west wind works against the ladders, and the shingles on the roof are coated with ice. Brenda is somewhere up by the top chimney. I sighted her from an upstairs window in the house next door. Grace assures us that Brenda has on a warm bathrobe, but the windchill factor makes it ten below. The chimney may be giving her some warmth. Wish I'd gotten here sooner." Jack shut up and looked to Oren and Latonya for help.

For once, her mouth failed Latonya. Blue's brother didn't say anything either. Policeman, veterinarian, and sister waited for Oren Bell to come up with an answer to how Brenda got on the roof and what to do to get her down. Oren knew the how and what to do.

"Brenda went up through a hole in the ceiling of Aunt Grace's bedroom closet." He explained this part easy. Latonya would have known it, if she wasn't so shocked out. "Once inside the attic, getting to the roof is a trick. There's no floor on the half of the attic next to the outside window. The window is only a narrow slit of half moon. Brenda must've gone across the beams and out through that little window. The three of us played up in the attic before Aunt Grace moved in. I never went out on the roof, but Brenda is light and quick and fearless."

"How did she carry the pup and the cat?" Jack asked.

"Most cats refuse to obey little girls, but Skid is like Spiro Spill. He follows Brenda. He goes where she goes. I suppose she held on to the puppy." Oren started up the steps to Aunt Grace's flat. Blue's brother, Jack, and Latonya heeled close behind him.

Latonya, out of her mind with worry, still felt duty bound

to warn them. "Aunt Grace requires all feet to remove shoes before stepping on the white carpeting."

Oren, Blue's brother, and Jack stomped on through with their shoes on, so Latonya did likewise.

As soon as they set foot in Aunt Grace's bedroom, Oren spotted the source of all the trouble. A newly scrubbed spot on Aunt Grace's pure white carpeting told where Tuffcity had last done his business. Oren played the scene through in his mind. That morning Latonya had locked the puppy downstairs in the kitchen before she took Brenda upstairs to Aunt Grace. Brenda must've sneaked down the back steps while Aunt Grace was watching *Love of Love* on television; and then his naughty little sister surely did carry Tuffcity back upstairs with her, with the old cat and Spiro tagging along. Aunt Grace hated new dogs, old cats, and friendly ghosts. Seeing a puppy spot on her carpeting would drive her crazy. Oren imagined fire coming out his aunt's ears and nose, mad screams out her mouth. About then, Brenda, pup, cat, and ghost clearly escaped up to the roof. High places didn't scare Brenda, but Aunt Grace did.

Oren stepped on Jack's shoulders and hoisted himself up into the black hole of the attic. Kicking his way through Aunt Grace's party dresses, Jack followed close behind. The big man was going to get himself stuck, and then how was Oren going to get Brenda and her friends back down through the hole?

Years of tenants had deposited unwanted junk up through the hole. Oren had been a younger kid when he last made a path amid the assorted treasures, but he knew the way. Jack, having successfully jackknifed his long frame full length into the attic, crawled behind Oren and supplied a needed light. They both had shed their outer garments in order to squeeze through the hole. Shivering from the stagnant cold, they moved toward the light from the half moon window.

"I'm scraping the skin off my belly," Jack whined.

The half moon lured Oren across the open rafters and over the waves of loose insulation.

"Oren, there's a big rat, looking right at me."

The rat was frozen dead and paying no attention to Jack. Oren concentrated on getting from one beam to the next. Jack kept coming behind him, holding the flashlight. They stopped at the window. The glass was broken. Jack was not going to get his big bulk through the small space.

"I have a rope," Jack offered.

"No rope." His words sounded unfriendly, but Oren was glad to have Jack behind him. He needed Jack's light. He needed a strong person as a backup to take Brenda, pup, and cat. Let Spiro go through the walls of the house by himself. Oren was the one to make the decisions here. Jack seemed to know this well enough. A board under the window gave Oren a shelf to surface his foot. The rotting wood groaned under his weight, but he refused to take his foot away. He needed the narrow ledge to raise and push himself out the window. The half moon opening was larger than he first thought. Praise the Lord for that much. Oren broke away the last dagger of window glass with his hand. He lifted himself quickly up and out, grabbing the top of the window for leverage. Once out, he braced his back against the side of the house. Feet apart, rubber soles gripping the icy bald shingles, snow swirls blinding his sight; he tried to think what to do next. If he looked down, there might be a net somewhere to catch a falling body, but better not to look down. The house next door leered at him, its red-eyed windows watching and waiting for him to falter and fall. The fascination of the house held his gaze for a long moment, but he came back to himself and his mission. Ignoring a sharp neck cramp, Oren looked up in the direction of the top chimney. He saw Brenda holding the pup tightly. Skid, a snow-covered blob, rested next to her. How had his little sister crawled up that solid sheet of ice? No matter, she'd done it. Now she sat still and steady, a wistful little dinosaur looking down on the icebergs.

"You see her, Oren?" Jack now had his big head out the half moon.

"I'll handle it, Jack." Oren heard the boards under Jack's feet give away. Sounds of old wood painfully breaking apart mingled with terrified human cursing. Oren held to his position. Let Jack take care of himself. If Oren didn't get Brenda down soon, he was going to fall off the roof and give the evil house next door its best laugh yet.

"Brenda Bell," Oren yelled through wind and snow, "I have come to save you." Brenda had not talked for days and he worried that she would refuse to talk now. He knew that she'd heard him.

Brenda broke her spoiled quiet spell. The trill of her fluty voice floated down to his ears. "I can't come down. I can't come down. If I come down, Aunt Grace will have the puppy put to sleep forever, and she will kick him first. Tuff-city, Skid, and me have decided to stay with the ship. Spiro's getting cold, so he's drifting on back to the purple room."

"Listen to me, Brenda. I have Jack behind me. Aunt

Grace is afraid of Jack. Blue's brother is here to protect Tuffcity. He will be safe in the arms of the law. Here's the plan. Pay attention. Brenda, you and the puppy slide true into my arms. Don't miss the mark, and we'll all be soon safe and warm together. Tell Skid to follow directly. Tell Skid we can't come back for him in an hour. It is now or never. Make it clear to him, Brenda." Oren knew that Skid liked to come and go in his own time.

For a long moment the sound of the wind filled up his ears and awareness. Oren wasn't sure if Brenda had heard his important instructions. The house next door watched and waited. Oren saw Brenda lean over and whisper into Skid's two upright ears, the only visible part of the snow-covered old cat. Then she shouted through the wind.

"I love you, Oren Bell. Get ready to receive us." Brenda hugged the puppy to her person. She put her feet out front like she was getting ready for a jolly winter slide.

Oren braced himself. Brenda knew how to calculate and be precise in her calculations. If he stayed firm against the house, she would hit him right on. Jack must be alive because he was making a ruckus behind the window. The crazy vet was up to something. With a sudden explosion, the entire section of the house behind Oren fell out. Jack was kicking with his big feet and pounding with an iron bedpost. Oren's back was now braced against nothing. Brenda shot directly toward him. He held rigid, squatting slightly like a person on skis, and he took his little sister and the puppy into his arms; they tumbled on top of Jack inside the attic of the old house. Jack had spread an old awning over the rafters. They lay together for a while, drawing security and warmth from each other.

"Skid won't come," Brenda broke the calm. "I told him that Oren wants him to come but he won't budge. Jack, you tell him to join us."

Jack covered them over with a piece of the awning, and then leaned out the open wound in the house and howled into the wind.

"Get down here immediately, you miserable, stubborn old cat. Kitteeee, kitteeee, come kitteeee."

Skid stretched, yawned, and delicately shook the snow off his coat—then with tail curled grandly over his back, he picked and pawed his way leisurely down the roof and entered the cavity of the house. The old cat settled on a beam and waited further direction.

"I think we are all here now. Lead us back, Oren." Jack gave the signal.

By the time they reentered the bedroom, Aunt Grace had covered her white carpeting with newspapers. They marched to the front door. Jack held Brenda tightly in his arms. Blue's brother carried Tuffcity. Oren and Skid brought up the rear.

Aunt Grace looked up from her television program. "A spoiled child and spoiled pets bring down misery on a household." She wagged a reproving finger at them.

Too wrung out to sass back, they muttered, "Afternoon, ma'am," and passed through.

Even hearing the story after the crisis was over shook Mama up. Brenda's head felt hot to her motherly touch, so Jack offered to take Mama and Brenda to Children's Hospital, just to be on the safe side. He knew a doctor there who would be glad to check Brenda over. Latonya and

Oren were given instructions to lock up and baby-sit themselves.

"Oren, I don't want to sleep by myself in the purple bedroom tonight. I believe that Spiro Spill went to the hospital with Brenda, Mama, and Jack. How 'bout me sleeping in the big chair by your sofa?"

"Sleep in the big chair if you want, Latonya, but I know that Spiro Spill still hides himself in the purple bedroom. Fred hit his last high note for him, and Spiro stayed on in the purple room. Spiro Spill is a fraidy-cat ghost. Brenda humors him and babies him. I think that Spiro should grow up and move on."

"When you're right, you're right, Oren. Brenda sleeps with one hand on Spiro's coattail, and where is he when she needs him? I hereby withdraw my support from that cowardly ghost. To change the subject, I felt proud to have you for my twin brother today. The way you took over the saving of Brenda was a miracle act of bravery."

"I saved her plenty of times before," Oren pointed out. "You always told me I deserved no credit for doing my job."

"The roof saving deserves extra credit," Latonya insisted. "I intend to give a full report to the entire seventh grade."

"There are only five people left in the seventh grade," Oren said drowsily. Skid was eager to get to sleep, and so was he.

"Oren, did you say your prayers yet?"

"I only say them twice a week," he confessed. "My friends who don't pray at all enjoy better luck than me."

"Shame on you, Oren Bell. The Lord needs your friendship and trust through bad times as well as good times. I'll start and you fall in."

"Dear Lord,
This is your friend, Latonya Bell.
This past week I let my soup slip.
Not a drop of love or nourishment
did I peel or plop into my pot.
Loved ones and hungry strangers
took away no substance from my kitchen
while I was crying and wailing in the puffed-up
pleasure
of my own sorry pride."

"Lord," Oren came in,
"My sister is a good girl.
Our mother and teacher know it to be true,
so you should know it too.
If Latonya carries on over Fred,
well, let her.
What do you expect, Lord?
I stirred the soup pot all week
and tossed in some greens and ribs.
Don't let Brenda's hunger strike fool you.
She ate some soup. I saw her."

"Lord," Latonya picked up the prayer again,
"I saw Brenda headed for a fall,
but I had to go to school
and leave my little sister with Aunt Grace,
who worships white carpeting."

Oren was determined to end the prayer.
"Brenda Bell is safely delivered up to Children's
Hospital.

In gratitude for Brenda
not falling off the Titanic,
Latonya and myself
agree to put up with Jack Daniels
if Mama wants him,
and if you hold him down, Lord,
to a couple of visits a week.
Amen."

"Oren," Latonya said sadly. "Why, do you think, did God let the house next door get Fred Lightfoot? Aunt Grace says that it happened because heaven needs trumpet players."

"Latonya, I hope the Lord doesn't think like Aunt Grace."

"What if Mama and Jack stay all night at the hospital with Brenda?" Latonya fussed on.

"I am here close by, Latonya. I am a very good people-saver, so rest easy and go to sleep."

Skid was asleep with his purr on automatic. Skid was a steady cat. Skid relaxed when danger was over and didn't worry about it before it happened, but still he was always properly nervous and alert and ready to defend himself against enemies. When Skid had a run of bad luck, he didn't demand for God to account. Skid appreciated a meal and a warm bed. When Jack Daniels handed him a decision of cancer, Skid just licked his lumps. Hey man, that Skid was one steady cat.

Chapter 13

o o o

Sunday morning plans included Oren and Latonya in a double hospital visit. The plan was first to call on Granddaddy at the Veterans Hospital in Allen Park, then head back to Detroit and spend time with Brenda at Children's Hospital.

"I don't know, Sarah," Jack said. "Why don't we all go together and see Brenda, then I can stop by the VA Hospital and see how Bill is doing later. I looked in on him yesterday and he is not a fit sight for children to see."

"We've been watching Granddaddy be 'not fit' long before you showed up, Jack Daniels," Oren said.

"Granddaddy's sickness will keep our minds off thinking about how we have to start up at Jefferson School on Monday morning," Latonya added.

Mama looked undecided. Oren and Latonya waited for Jack to give the final word on the subject. Oren noted that they'd been doing that a lot lately.

"I vote for skipping church," Jack said, "and having breakfast at the Pancake House, then like a family, we'll go to visit Brenda and Bill."

Mama went from undecided to mildly miffed. Jack frequently found ways to skip church, and Aunt Grace was depending on them for a ride to morning worship.

"We'll skip church," Mama compromised, "but we'll deliver Grace and her children to the church door." Mama always made little deals with Jack and they both got satisfaction from it.

All of the old soldiers and sailors who suffered with Granddaddy's disease were housed together on one floor of the VA Hospital. Oren hoped to find Bill Bell dressed in his new Christmas robe, sitting up straight, watching his little television set, maybe philosophizing and giving out free advice to the other sick veterans. Such was not the scene. Granddaddy lay flat upon his bed. He resembled a drained out, dried-up old shell of his former self. He had looked better when he was flushed full of Red Rose wine. It took Bill a while to get his eyes open. He glanced sullenly at his family. Jack was the only one he wanted to talk to and was the one responsible for putting him where he was.

"Damn, Jack. I want you to get me out of this buggy place."

"They told me that you are coming along fine," Jack said.

"Don't you believe it," Granddaddy gasped. "Last night two ugly nurses tied me to my bed. I always did hate ugly nurses. They don't come when you call them. What's worse, all the doctors working here are near to a hundred years old. When the time comes for broken-down docs to be let out to pasture, they send them all here."

"The staff seems to me to be in their prime," Jack said, although the docs looked pretty old to Oren.

"Don't you believe it," Granddaddy said. "Another thing, this hospital allows elephants to walk around inside my room at night. Old doctors and old nurses with their old eyes can't see the filthy beasts."

"Do the elephants bother you, Bill?" Jack went along, but Oren seriously doubted if there were any real elephants around. Sometimes Granddaddy saw things that weren't there.

"Do they bother me? The dirty brutes do their business on the floor beside my bed. When the ugly nurses do decide to let me out of bed, I might step in an elephant poop pie. I don't call that a clean way to run a hospital. Speak to the head old doctor, Jack. Get me out of here. I'll slip you five bucks for your trouble."

"I'll see what I can do, Bill," Jack lied.

Mama and Latonya appeared uncomfortable, and Jack wanted to get them out and away. It didn't make that much difference, because Granddaddy wasn't paying them any attention.

"We'll come back soon—when you're feeling better," Jack said.

"Can I stay for a while?" Oren asked. It made him mad to have to plead with Jack to talk to his own grandfather.

Jack waited to see how Mama felt. When Mama nodded,

he said, "We'll be downstairs in the coffee shop, Oren. Don't stay too long. We still have to visit Brenda."

When they were alone, Granddaddy stopped grumbling about elephants and went to sleep. Oren watched him sleep until fifteen minutes had passed by on his new watch that Jack had given him. He was about to get up and leave, when Bill woke up and examined him with clear eyes.

"That you, Oren?

"It's me, Granddaddy."

"What's happening?"

"Brenda is sick in the hospital, but she's getting better. She climbed up on the roof, and me and Jack had to go up and bring her down."

"That's good. Are the puppy and cat all right?"

"The puppy hasn't had an accident in a while. Skid is holding his own, but he misses you. Granddaddy, Fred Lightfoot was murdered in the house next door. I know about the steamer operation. Was that why the house got him?"

Granddaddy didn't appear all that surprised or horrified. He thought a minute and said, "Steamer operation wasn't all there was to it. Fred ran and fetched for whoever paid him a buck to do so. He worked both sides of the hall. He knew more than he should about a lot of deals. I knew a horn player in Vegas like him once. He was named Slink. Slink lived to grow older than Fred."

"Tell me what Fred knew," Oren pressed.

"Then you'll know too much."

Oren wasn't sure he wanted to know too much, so he let that one go. "Granddaddy, did they pay you for burning their criminal records?"

"They paid me in cheap wine. They figured I was too burned out to read what I burned. They figured I couldn't remember my own name. There's times when I can't. Burning their junk was my hobby, but I get my big money from Spiro and the house. Hell, we're family to Spiro. We got Spiro's money coming to us."

Bill Bell dropped off like a shot into a deep sleep, and there was no waking him. Oren knew if he did succeed in rousing him, Bill would more than likely be back into elephants. How much of his grandfather's talk could he believe? How could Bill be getting money from Spiro and the house?

Chapter 14

o   o   o

Ⅰt was early afternoon when the Bells and Jack reached Children's Hospital. They took the elevator right up to Brenda's floor. While Mama and Jack checked on Brenda's condition at the desk, Oren and Latonya sat together in the family reception area.

"Oren," Latonya whispered, "everywhere I look I see suffering little children. I never saw so many in one place before."

"I never gave it much thought." Oren kept his voice low, so as not to offend the suffering children. His eyes rested on the wall in front of them. Pinned up on a board was a picture by Brenda Bell. Brenda had been in the hospital less than a week, and most of that time she'd had tubes in her nose. How did she find the time? This Crayola picture was a new and bigger *Titanic,* in full tilt.

Jack came back from the desk and took them to Brenda's room. Oren expected to see Brenda laid low by her serious illness, maybe still a bit pouty and silent. Not so. Their little sister was pleased and peppy to see them. In the center of a six-bed ward, she beamed out in all directions. There was a little girl who looked like she might be blind sitting on the end of Brenda's bed. There was a lady standing in attendance. A boy sat in a wheelchair beside her bed. Brenda could find boyfriends anywhere she happened to be. Latonya was not as good at attracting boyfriends.

"This is one of my newest best friends, Henry Greenberg," Brenda introduced.

"Hello there, son," cool Jack said. "Do you play baseball?"

How stupid could a grown man be, asking a kid in a wheelchair if he played baseball?

"This is Janey, another new best friend, and this is Dr. Mary Herbert. She is helping to make me well."

"Brenda is getting ready to tell one of her stories," the doctor told them. "I'll round up a couple of chairs for you folks."

"Mama, Jack, Oren, Latonya, I am getting ready to tell my famous God Story to my new friends. You guys can help me because you know it so well."

"Brenda, do you think that is a good idea?" Mama was very serious. Oren knew that his mama was afraid the God Story might drain Brenda. It wouldn't. Brenda loved telling the story. Mama was embarrassed by hearing the story told out loud to strangers in the presence of Jack Daniels. She should be.

"I'd like to hear it," Jack said. Jack was always up for hearing stories about their family.

"I'm looking forward to hearing it," Dr. Herbert said.

"Please tell it," Janey said.

"I bet it's about the *Titanic,*" Henry Greenberg guessed.

"I'll help you, Brenda," Latonya offered.

Oren wasn't all that sure the God Story had really happened, but then he couldn't even see Spiro Spill. Brenda had made up the God Story before she knew about the *Titanic,* but she would probably add a few *Titanic* particulars to the plot. When Brenda had a good audience her God Story grew. Latonya was a believer in Brenda's story, but Latonya believed most anything. Propped up by pillows, Brenda was ready, and as bright as a new copper penny. She took a deep breath and started.

"Oren Bell and other doubters tell me that they don't know what God looks like. If anybody here doesn't know, listen to me and you will know for ever after. God spreads around and above the world, a giant so high that the sun warms his belly and the oceans splash his toes."

"Is God a man giant?" the lady doctor asked.

"Oren and Latonya are boy and girl twins, God is both boy and girl in one. I call him he, because I want to." Brenda's answer seemed to satisfy.

"Brenda, how do you know God is higher than the sun?" Henry Greenberg said. "You can't see up that high."

If they didn't stop picking away at the unimportant parts of the story, how was Brenda going to get to the good parts? As long as she was telling it, Oren liked to hear it told smooth, with no interruptions.

"I am high-sighted when I look at God," Brenda explained patiently. "Once I saw God standing over the Lodge Freeway. It was after a rainstorm. He shimmered in all the colors of the rainbow, but firmed into a form for me to see. Aunt Grace says human persons are forbidden to gaze full in the face of God, but I did and he didn't seem to mind. He knew that I was Brenda Bell from Detroit, Michigan. I stood still and we looked back and forth at each other. I felt warm and smart and loved. It was the greatest feeling. I believe that God felt better for looking at me, but he had to move off in the direction of the Windsor Tunnel."

"Did you ever see God when your eyes were closed?" Janey asked.

"My best God sighting came to me when I had my eyes closed," Brenda told them. "It happened when I was a little girl too small to go to school. Latonya, you tell this part of the story, so I can rest my voice."

Latonya took over gladly. "Brenda's first God sighting occurred before we lived in our present home on Fourth Street. We lived in a one-room hotel apartment over on Cass Avenue. We never left the room because we were afraid to. Our whole world was in that one room. When our daddy felt like showing up, he made our mama sad, but still we needed him to buy us food and pay for the room. Mama couldn't leave us to find work. One night Brenda accused our world of being ugly. She turned her face to the wall, closed her eyes and said that she never wanted to see our world again. At times, spoiled spells come over our little sister. Mama kept urging her to taste some Campbell's chicken soup, but she refused. We were so worried over her. You tell the rest, Brenda. Your spoiled spells make me mad."

Brenda continued the story. "When I closed my eyes and turned my head to the wall, there he was, big as life."

"God," Janey guessed.

"Right," Brenda continued. "I had to look at him because I couldn't turn around and face the world. God spoke to me in a booming voice. He said, 'I MADE THE LAND AND SEAS AND ALL THE CREATURES. DON'T TURN AWAY FROM MY WORLD, BRENDA BELL.' Well, I have such a sassy mouth, I said, 'Oh, God, did you make the Cass Hotel and all the creatures in it?' "

"What did he have to say to that?" Jack wanted to know. Jack had never heard any good stuff like he was now hearing.

"God proclaimed the Cass Hotel to be the work of man, but he did admit to making the cockroaches. Then he lifted me up in front of his shining face, so we could better see and hear each other. 'BRENDA BELL,' he said, 'I WILL SHOW YOU MY BEAUTIFUL WORLD AND CREATURES, THEN YOU'D BETTER GET BACK TO YOUR UGLY WORLD AND MAKE IT BETTER. AT LEAST, DO THE BEST THAT YOU CAN.' 'Sure, sure,' I said, getting a little tired of all God's big talk. 'Show me, God.' "

"Does God have wings like an angel?" Janey presented her own private picture.

"I bet," Henry Greenberg said, "that God was like Superman flying over the world with Brenda in his arms, like she was Lois Lane."

"No wings like an angel or flying like Superman," Brenda

146

said. "God put me inside his head, so I could look out of his eyes. If he wanted me to be inside the head of another creature, he arranged it. It was easy for him to do."

"Neat," Henry said.

"I never get tired of hearing this part of the story," Oren said. He was glad that he knew what was coming.

Brenda took a deep breath and let them have it.

> *"First, God let me be a hawk.*
> *I spread my hawk wings and soared above the earth.*
> *Little creatures running around and hiding below*
> *looked like food for me,*
> *but I wasn't hungry and wanted to go even higher,*
> *so I became an eagle*
> *and soared above the mountains.*
> *Then I dropped down to the earth*
> *to become a horse.*
> *I shook my head and snorted and pawed the*
>   *ground,*
> *while meek little creatures I couldn't see*
> *scattered beneath my feet.*
> *Then I changed into pure knowing*
> *and cast my all-seeing eyes to the far north water.*
> *While perched on the peakiest part of the world,*
> *I saw the space where all the white snow is stored*
>   *up.*
> *With little ice stones stinging my spirit cheek,*
> *I spied the floating ice hill that ripped open a ship.*
> *Then quickly*
> *I drifted down to low, dry, hot land*
> *so I could make the rain fall where it was needed.*

Creatures fell to their knees and blessed me for my
  effort.
God made me into a mother lion
and I stalked food for my hungry babies
but I didn't hate the food I hunted
and God blessed the graceful creatures when they
  fell.
I wished to look a mountain eye to eye,
so I became a mountain goat.
Together God and I delighted in the morning
and watched the sun go down.
I drank water from the springs that made the seas
and I swam upstream with a very nice salmon.
For a while
I was busy in the world of ants and bees."

"Brenda," Latonya stopped her, "creatures and sunsets are nice, but get to the part about the suffering people."

"We saw plenty of people suffering," Brenda granted. "Once God blew off a mountain top because he knew it was time for him to blow. The insides of the mountain ran down the outside and covered a town of people. God and me saw one little girl still alive and struggling, so we pushed her to safety. We didn't know if the little girl was good or bad, or even if she believed in us or not. For a while, God and I watched a war. It wasn't us who made it happen. It wasn't the worst sight we saw. Dipping down to the street corners of the Cass Corridor in Detroit, Michigan, finally we moved up and down the halls of the Cass Hotel. God sadly agreed with me that my world was worse than most. He told me to go back and comfort my mama, my sister, and my brother. He told me not to sulk so much. I put it to him square. How do you expect a small girl to make a dump like that any better? God said, 'BEAR UP AND STAND FIRM, BRENDA BELL.' I whined and said, 'Send me some miracles. Please. I know you can do it.' "

It was quiet as they all waited for the end of the story. That Brenda Bell sure knew how to talk to God.

The story continued. "God gave such a deep breath that his sigh blew out a star. 'VERY WELL, BRENDA BELL,' he gave in. 'YOU CAN HAVE FIVE ORDINARY, EVERYDAY MIRACLES TO HELP YOUR FAMILY ALONG, AND ONE SPECIAL MIRACLE THAT BELONGS TO YOU ALONE.'

"I said, 'thank you very much. I love you, God.' He said, 'YOU'RE WELCOME. I LOVE YOU, BRENDA BELL.' Then he was gone, so I went to sleep. When I woke up in the morning I knew it was the day for the first miracle. Latonya and Oren were sitting together staring out the window. Poor things, they thought our small ugly world was going to last forever. Mama measured out some cereal into our bowls. We didn't have any milk to cover it up. When a knock came at our door, I knew our first miracle had arrived. Latonya and Oren feared it might be our daddy. Mama also feared it might be him, but she opened the door anyway. Standing there, we saw Bill Bell for the very first time. Even then he was full of Red Rose wine. He said that he was the bearer of good news. He said our daddy had taken off for another state, and didn't want us anymore. He said, no son of Betty Bell was worth a fret or a backward thought. He gave us his last ten dollars. We spent the money for bologna, milk, and ice cream. Granddaddy had withheld enough for a bottle of Red Rose wine. That night, I went to bed happy because I knew that other miracles would come in time. Sure enough, the next day, the second miracle turned up. Granddaddy took care of Oren, Latonya, and me, while Mama went out to look for a job. She found one at the J. L. Hudson Company. The job paid good money and had benefits. The third miracle came soon after. One of Mama's new friends at the J. L. Hudson Company told her about our present grand and beautiful house. It was all condemned, empty, and waiting for us to move in. Condemned is not a good word, but we have lived in our condemned house for three years. Aunt Grace moved into the upstairs flat of our house, but that was not a miracle."

"What was the next miracle?" Jack asked. He was holding Mama's hand and looking sappy.

"We bought a television set on easy time payments."

Jack was surprised that a television set rated as a full miracle, but it was one of Oren's favorites.

"The next miracle," Brenda continued, "was finding Spiro Spill lurking in the corner of our purple bedroom. Being kind of purple himself, he wasn't easy to spot. His spirit was fast fading into nothing, and he needed immediate attention. My sister, Latonya, helped me save that poor ghost."

"It was nice of your family to be kind to a ghost," Henry Greenberg appreciated. "But Brenda, what was the sixth and special miracle just for you?"

"The special miracle was a gift from God, but I found out about it from the television set. One day while Granddaddy and me were home alone watching *Sesame Street,* we discovered that I am a number genius."

"Brenda," Oren said, "tell your friends why this gift is so great. Not everybody thinks that numbers are beautiful, not even me."

"If I use my special gift well, I can sit on high with astronauts, engineers, or C.P.A.s. What's more, beautiful numbers can ease the suffering in the world as well as beautiful words. My mama says so. My Granddaddy says so, and God says so too."

"Makes sense to me," the lady doctor said.

The God Story was over and Brenda was tired. Jack helped Janey and Henry Greenberg return to their beds. Almost before Mama stopped kissing Brenda, Oren's little sister fell asleep.

In the car, Mama reminded Jack that Aunt Grace was home in the downstairs flat, preparing Sunday dinner for them. Pot roast, mind you.

"Why is she doing that?" Jack demanded peevishly.

"To be nice," Mama said, "and she wants to comfort us."

"Comfort us for what?" Jack said.

Mama looked to Latonya and they nodded their girl heads, like it was something that Oren and Jack couldn't understand. Oren eased himself over to Jack's side of the car, and they communicated eye to eye, man to man. Jack winked at him, and it gave them both satisfaction.

Chapter 15

○   ○   ○

Jefferson School turned out to be a total disaster for Latonya. The house was getting Oren by hurting his sisters.

"We have to wait by the bus for Latonya," Oren insisted to Blue and Whitey. "Jefferson School is driving her down."

"How's that?" Blue asked.

He had explained it the day before when Blue had asked him the same question. Blue couldn't remember one thing, unless he forgot something first to give it room. Oren repeated patiently, "Latonya is going down in her schoolwork and this makes her low spirited. She needs friends to rally around her, and I promised my mother that we'd do it."

"I'm not high on Jefferson School myself," Whitey said.

"What kind of school chooses Dink Bell to be student of the day, then puts a star on his forehead for doing nothing? The kid's going to have stars all over his face by the time the week is out."

Blue added, "How 'bout that teacher who pops candies in your mouth when you come up with a right answer? Jefferson teachers accept all answers as right answers. They want us to develop tooth decay and a have good self-image. Who needs a self-image?"

Latonya joined them. She was trying to put on a happy face. It made her look sick, but at least she didn't throw up. Oren promised himself that he'd be nice to his sister for the rest of his life, but he could never tell her that he had opened an eye during the ceremony. A shifty and ordinary type, like himself, knew how to get along at Jefferson School. Latonya would never fit in. They had only been at the new school for a few days, but by the way Latonya was moving, she might as well forget medical school.

The four refugees from Spiro Spill Elementary sat together at the back of the bus. There were some ugly bigger kids hogging the middle seats. Dink's stars didn't give him protection and neither did Latonya, so he and Dede stayed up front by the driver. Now was the time for Oren to bring up the subject. There was noise enough on the bus to make them feel like they were alone.

"How about if we explore the house next door when we get off the bus? Check it out." Oren waited.

"You crazy?" Blue and Whitey asked together.

"You don't mean me?" Latonya counted herself out. "And you had better not mean them and you, Oren. The house next door has been serving the needs of men who steal cars, move cocaine, and murder innocent children. It's all I can do to pass it twice a day, going to and coming from the corner. I thank goodness that we are protected by the ceremony. That house deserves to be hated and I hate it, but I would never taunt it because I know its power."

"Look, Latonya," Oren said. "The house next door has been cleared out by the police department and they have it under surveillance. That house is safer than most houses in Detroit right now. If they tear it down soon, like they say they might, well, then, we'll never get a chance to go inside and look around."

"Curiosity killed a cat, Oren. Why do we need to go inside and look around an evil house?"

"Not for curiosity," Oren insisted. "Granddaddy hinted to me that there might be some treasure meant for us. If Spiro stashed something away that is not hammered into the walls, it belongs to us. If we go in now, there will still be daylight. Evil has no power in the daylight. You said that yourself, Latonya, many times."

"I always wanted to give that house an inside look," Blue admitted. "If me and Whitey share the danger, can we share in the treasure?"

"Sure, Blue. Me and Latonya aren't greedy."

Latonya grimly mulled it over. "Brenda told me there was a treasure," she finally admitted. "Brenda said that Spiro wanted us to have it."

That was news to Oren, but he believed it. Spiro told Brenda everything.

When the bus let them off at the corner, they didn't speak to each other. Somehow an agreement without words had been reached. Oren, Blue, and Whitey had been talking about going inside the house for three years; so now they were going to do it. Oren was the leader because Fred was gone. Besides, Oren had been inside the house before. Funny how he didn't feel afraid. He felt eager to get on with it. Maybe this time he would be able to reverse the reverse curse.

The door that had admitted him on his first trip inside the house was boarded over and locked, by order of the Detroit police department.

"There are loose boards on one of the basement windows," Latonya pointed out.

For a law-abiding person like Latonya to ignore the warning TRESPASSERS WILL BE PROSECUTED TO THE FULL EXTENT OF THE LAW must be pure hell, but she was supporting their crime all the way.

Most of the boards on the windows had been recently reinforced, but the one spotted by Latonya was covered with clinging weeds. The weeds and rotten wood yielded easily to Blue's pocket knife.

"Oren, we don't have a light to take in with us." Whitey was wavering at the portal of evil. "The boards will shut out all the daylight."

"There will be enough light," Oren assured them, but he wasn't sure. He needed to talk bold to keep up their spirits.

They dropped through the window one by one, and landed on some kind of a workbench. So far, so good.

"Hardly no light at all," Blue muttered.

"When our eyes get used to the darkness, we'll see what we need to see," Oren insisted, but he didn't believe it.

Holding on to each other, they stumbled through the many rooms in the basement.

"What are we looking for?" Whitey asked.

"I don't think it would be jewels or hundred-dollar bills," Latonya said. "It would have to be something that only Granddaddy recognized as having value, and it would be something that he could easily hock."

They came into the main room of the basement, and there was enough light coming through the cracks in the window boards for them to admire the splendor. A magnificent pool table dominated the shadowy room. No electricity was working, but Latonya found a fancy candle holder filled with candles. Oren had matches in his pocket, so they each took a candle to carry and light the way.

"Who would have thought Spiro would've had a pool table," Blue said.

"Spiro was a trumpet player," Latonya reminded them. "The pool table was put here by the bootleggers. Brenda told me what belonged to who."

"Latonya," Blue put to her, "how do you know that Spiro doesn't hang around this house? Maybe he is not as scared as you think. He might like this house. It's grander than your house."

"He might," Latonya admitted. "Even Brenda can't account for Spiro's comings and goings every blessed minute. Lead on, Oren. I feel my old fears of this place falling away."

He led them single file, holding their candles, up the steps through the kitchen into the center hall.

"Where do you think the treasure's at, Oren?" Blue asked. "It's cold as a tomb and dead quiet inside this place."

"I never heard such quiet before," Whitey agreed.

As if to oblige Blue and Whitey, faint sounds came from

the upper reaches of the house. They looked up to where the stairs disappeared into the shadows.

"I think I hear music," Latonya said, her voice calm enough, considering what they were hearing.

"Let's get out of here," Whitey said.

"When I was here before," Oren tried to calm them, "I heard music and I followed it. It turned out to be natural music."

"Did it sound like this music, Oren?" Blue inquired.

"No, it sounded like a scratchy marching band. This music sounds like church music, but I'm sure it will be natural when we find it."

"You think we should follow this music?" Latonya looked to Oren.

"Why not?"

"Then lead on, Oren. We are right behind you."

The second floor was a long hallway of closed doors, with the dirty nose of a window at the end letting in muddy rays of orange. The staircase swept grandly up to the third floor. In the Bell–Spill house, a person had to go through a hole in the ceiling to get to the third floor. Spiro really outdid himself in building his new house. The music was coming from the third floor. With no discussion, they followed Oren up the stairs.

"Don't stand so close to me," Oren warned Latonya. "You're burning my hair with your candle."

Only one door stood at the top of the stairs, and the music here was powerful. Oren paused a moment and then turned the knob. It opened easily. The music stopped. Oren and Latonya entered boldly. Blue and Whitey followed.

The third floor was one big room, the walls plastered and

the ceiling peaked like a church. The red windows threw out a bloody energy to all the space and corners. The only furniture was a pipe organ that appeared to be built into the heavy oak woodwork, secured safely beneath the watchful eyes of the red windows.

"Something was playing that organ, and it stopped when we came in," Blue said.

"You'd think an organ like this would have got ripped off," Whitey said in a hushed tone.

"Strong thieves with a truck couldn't get that big pipe organ loose and out and down the stairs. The door isn't wide enough to let it through, and the house keeps what it wants." Latonya's reasoning made sense.

"Who was playing it?" Oren asked.

"Oren, I do believe that Spiro followed us over. I bet he wanted us to hear and see his organ. Getting it up and in must have been a victory for him. He may have been only third on the trumpet, but he sure plays the organ good."

"I'm glad there is a natural reason for the music." Oren accepted Latonya's explanation. They weren't afraid of Spiro in their own house, so why should he bother them in this house? Spiro had a right to be in either place. The thing that bothered Oren was this: Spiro was no match for this house. It had done him in once, and it could do them all in, if it wanted.

"Do you think that the treasure is here, Oren?" Blue was eager to leave. "I'm dying of cold and the red eyes are making me nervous."

"I don't think that the treasure is here," Oren said. "And I think Spiro slid by us when we came in."

Whitey's candle went out while they shivered and waited for Oren to tell them what to do.

"Granddaddy came inside the house many times, but he wouldn't be apt to cruise around. Even if he heard music upstairs, he wouldn't bother to follow it. That's not Granddaddy's style. He'd stay in the parlor in front of the fireplace where he had business to be. If there's any treasure, he'd stumble on it accidentally. Spiro would nearly have to put it in Granddaddy's hand before he'd spot it."

"Then let's go to the parlor," Blue and Whitey said, like they had one mind between them.

"Those red windows are a treasure," Latonya said, as they took a last look.

"Let's get down, Latonya," Blue urged. "Before the house takes hold of us."

"Don't worry, Blue. I trust that we are protected by the ceremony."

Oh, great! Oren led the way back down. In the beginning, Latonya's ceremony had been pure nincompoopery, but her belief had made it real as rain.

"Blue," Whitey squeaked. "Where was it that you said the cops found Fred's body?"

"Inside a second-floor room."

They lifted their candles and gave pause to look down the dark corridor of the second floor where Fred Lightfoot had met his end. Which door? Oren smelled the ghost smell but he kept it to himself.

"Latonya, why do you think this house practices and attracts evil?" Whitey moved closer to Latonya, who could be counted on to give off answers and protection.

"Hard to say," Latonya said.

"I heard from reliable sources that murder and evil deeds hang on where they happen," Whitey said.

"That is not true of this house," Latonya disallowed. "The evil was here before the people."

They huddled now in the downstairs center hall. The gold-leaf paper was torn and the light fixture had been ripped off, but the hallway held on to its smug and courtly beauty. It looked a lot better than it smelled.

"Latonya, do you think that the house was built on a haunted bog or over an old graveyard?" Oren presented what he believed to be the best possibility.

"Could be," Latonya said.

"I think that the bootleggers finished the second floor out of wood from cursed trees," Blue said. "Brenda says that wood infested by druid spirits doomed the *Titanic* while she was being built."

"Evil has many ways of seeping in and taking hold of a place, but there are always powers to save." Latonya closed the subject. "Now, lead on, Oren."

The parlor fireplace had some paper and wood waiting to be lit, so they lit it. Oren figured that smoke coming out of the chimney would attract attention, but they were near to freezing, so they had to take the chance.

"Where do we look, Oren?" Latonya asked, walking over to the gramophone. The old music machine sat securely on a high cabinet. There on shelves were stacked piles of big, flat, old records. She took out a pile.

"They're not even dusty," she marvelled.

Blue and Whitey started pounding up and down the walls looking for secret openings and knocking new holes in the plaster. Oren pried at loose bricks around the fire-place.

"These old records might be worth some money"—Latonya held one up—"but hocking ordinary old records is not Granddaddy's style. Still, he took the time to dust them off." She ran her finger up and down the pile on her lap. "Wait a minute. Spiro is putting my mind and hand on to something. Alleluia." Latonya exhibited what looked like a solid-gold record. "There may be more. They are shuffled in so you can't see them unless you're searching. I couldn't see the shimmer till I took away the others, although Grand-daddy might have found them someplace else and put them in with the other records. He likes to keep his trea-sures where he can get at them."

"You think Spiro's Sousa group got a gold record for the Washington Post March?" Oren asked.

"I think that Spiro took real gold given to him by his rich wife, and had it molded into the shape of records," Latonya said as she continued going through the old records look-ing for more glint.

"I wonder who Enrico Caruso was?" Oren gave his sister a hand with the records, without expecting an answer.

They found four gold records. Each of them put one under their coat. If there were more, the four searchers were searched out.

"Let's hold on to these for a while," Oren said. "It's not like we're ripping off something that belongs to the house. Spiro gave enough of his gold away to children and sick people. This is our special gold."

"How do we know it's gold?" Blue asked.

"Because Granddaddy had real money in his horn. Do

you think it's honest for us to keep them, Latonya?" Oren went to the authority on honesty.

"It's very borderline, Oren, but I vote that we hold on to them for a while. Now lead us out of this evil-smelling place."

Halfway across the empty lot, they looked back. The house gazed back at them like a wounded beast.

Mama was home early, and she did not encourage Blue and Whitey to hang around. The minute they were out the door, Mama sat Oren and Latonya down for a serious talk. Oren suspected hard news, and when he suspected hard news, it was bound to happen.

"We have to move out of our home," she told them. "We received our move-on notice from the city." She took a breath and continued. "In three weeks the doors will close at the downtown J. L. Hudson Company."

"But Mama," Latonya said, "the J. L. Hudson Company covers two blocks on Woodward Avenue. How can they close it down? Where will it go? It is so tall and so beautiful."

"They say it will be made into a parking structure."

"Is Jack coming by to take us to the hospital to see Brenda?" Oren asked. He knew the steady answer to that one, but he wanted to lighten Mama's mood.

"I don't think so." Mama gave them the final shock. "Jack and I have had a little disagreement. He may not be coming by anymore."

Even a positive thinker like Latonya couldn't think up anything worth holding on to. Maybe now was the time to tell his sister that he had opened his eyes during the ceremony. Then she'd know who was really to blame.

Chapter 16

○ ○ ○

The morning after finding the treasure, Blue and Whitey missed the school bus. Latonya thought they might have caught a chill from their adventure inside the house. Latonya said she felt a little chilly herself. She recovered during social studies and was able to present the new teacher with one of her original ideas. Teachers from the first grade on had always appreciated Latonya's ideas. Even Miss Bobb had liked them well enough. This Jefferson teacher looked confused and offended over his sister's offering; and then she ignored Latonya and gave the nod to another kid who said something the teacher liked better. Oren wished that he'd been paying attention and heard what it was that Latonya had said. It couldn't have been anything dirty. Having been rejected by a teacher, his poor sister went back into her down funk. She kept her mouth shut for the rest of the day.

He waited for Latonya after school. Together they took the last two side-by-side seats on the bus. She was quiet.

"Wanna talk?" Oren said.

"About what?"

He dipped around inside his head for a subject outside the house next door.

"You know what it was that Mama and Jack had their falling out over?"

Latonya gave this some thought. "Their fights aren't loud and mean like the ones Mama used to have with Daddy. I don't think Jack hits women. He does act childish sometimes, like most men do. I heard Mama say to him that he was neglecting his animals and job duties by driving in to see her so often; and just maybe it would be best for the two of them to cool it for a while. Jack says back to her, if she don't want to see him every day, maybe it would be better if he didn't come around at all. That's the way Mama and Jack fight. Mama is into being a new woman and not taking guff from a man."

They passed the house next door without looking at it. Oren settled down on the porch steps, letting Latonya enter the flat ahead of him. Their days in the comfortable old house were numbered. Latonya went through to check out the rooms, and she needed time alone to feel the familiar spaces. Oren prepared himself for a wait, pulling his hood over his head to shut out the cold wind. Latonya was back in less time than it took for him to freeze.

"Oren," she said, her voice quivering, "Aunt Grace is waiting for us in our living room because she wants to comfort us. She tells me that a big city truck was working on the house next door all morning. She thinks that when they backed out, the truck ran over Skid. She heard a cat go screeching off. Aunt Grace says that old cats always go off by themselves to die. She says the city men were taking an organ and a pool table out in pieces." Latonya sat down on the steps beside him.

Oren opened his mouth but no words came out. He tried to rise up but his body wouldn't work. The house was paying them back again. They couldn't win a lick against it. The house was blaming them for the loss of the organ and pool table. It wasn't their fault, but that spiteful house had to blame somebody. Now Skid was suffering because he was their cat. Latonya pulled Oren to his feet and started hugging him like she was a bear. The shock of being hugged by Latonya brought him to his senses.

"Oren, don't give out on me. We'll find him. He must be hiding in the high weeds around the house next door. C'mon." She went ahead, calling, "Skideeeeeeee, Skideeeeeeee."

Halfway between their house and the house next door, they heard Skid's voice weakly calling to them.

"Here he is, Oren. You pick him up. You are more gentle than me at picking up hurt creatures."

Oren lifted the victim carefully, supporting Skid from nose to tail. Latonya went ahead to clear a path and open doors. Oren placed Skid, like a dying king, on the bed in the purple bedroom. Aunt Grace followed them in, Tuffcity nipping at her heels.

"That old cat has cancer anyway," Aunt Grace comforted. "I heard how old sick cats throw themselves beneath

the wheels of trucks to save themselves from more suffering. Let me call the cops and have Skid shot. It's the kindest
thing we can do for him. I'll tell the cops not to send Blue's
brother. He is no good at shooting."

"We'll wait for our own vet," Oren Bell told her, not
knowing if Jack would show.

Aunt Grace went back upstairs, because she didn't like
meeting up with Jack Daniels. Oren and Latonya sat on the
bed, Skid between them. They waited and watched. Oren
stroked under Skid's chin. The old cat managed to purr
right through his pain.

"Latonya, do you think Jack will come?"

"It's half past four o'clock now. Jack teaches a class of
student vets in the morning hours. He treats animals at the
clinic in the afternoon hours. If there are no emergencies to
hold him, he could be on the road by this time. I'll put some
water in a spoon. Oren, you try to get Skid to take a drop.
Look at him laying there so cute and trusting. He doesn't
know Mama and Jack are at odds."

Blue's mother called at five o'clock. She wanted to know
about the golden record. She said Blue had one. He
thought he was being cursed by it, and he was sick with
worry over the house getting him. Blue's mother wanted to
talk to their mother. Latonya told Mrs. Brown that their
mother was obliged to visit Brenda in the hospital after her
workday was over, and she wouldn't be home until late. A
bigger emergency than golden records had come up, so
Latonya advised Mrs. Brown to tell Blue to stay cool.

Oren and Latonya sat together on the bed and watched
Skid.

"Look, Oren," Latonya broke the silence. "There is Spiro cowering in the corner. You always wanted to see him. There he is."

His eyes followed Latonya's pointing finger. The setting sun floated shadows on the ceiling, chased shapes up and down the walls. It was the time of day for ghostly forms to come alive and briefly have their flicker. Oren thought that he could see their ghost.

"Latonya, is Spiro causing our bad luck? Is Spiro waiting for Skid to die? Is Spiro part of the house?"

"That is the dumbest thing that you have ever said, Oren. Spiro is worrying over Skid just like you and me. Spiro is family. He wanted the house next door to be a place for happy times. How do you think he feels having his organ all busted up and taken out in pieces?"

They both heard a car stop, a car door slam, footsteps missing the broken step. Was it a cop come to shoot Skid out of his misery? Was it Fred's murderer? Most times Oren and Latonya knew the sound of Jack's car, but now they were too upset to take anything for granted. No knocking on the door. Jack had a key. Latonya ran off to identify the visitor. Her glad hooting told Oren that Jack had not deserted them. Latonya never was one to hold back. Oren kept on stroking Skid. Sometimes Jack put injured and sick animals to sleep. He had done it before and he would do it again. Oren's head ached from not crying.

Jack kneeled by the bed to examine Skid. Skid trusted Jack and didn't complain. Skid was a very brave cat. Jack stroked Skid's head, a decision creasing his brow.

"What do you think, Jack?" Oren expected the worse.

"I think the truck backed over Skid's tail," Jack said.

"We'll take him to the University Veterinary Hospital in Lansing and X-ray him for internal injuries. I'll need to amputate his tail for sure. The tail is causing Skid distress."

"Will he live without a tail?" Oren held his breath, not able to let go until he heard the verdict.

"He'll have to retire from the alley and be a full-time house cat, but he can live without a tail. I am not sure if he can survive the surgery, but we will try."

There was a big fuss when Mama got home. Whitey's mother had called her at her work. There was no time for explanations with Skid to worry over, but Mama demanded an explanation about the gold records. Latonya explained. Mama wasn't happy about them finding the treasure. She was angry that they had gone inside the house without her permission. Even Latonya knew that they would never have gotten permission to go inside the house. It was Jack who finally got things back on track. Old Jack knew what was important. He said that Skid could die while they were all going on about the house and the gold records. He said that they needed to sit down and plot a course of action. Mama agreed, so that's what they did. It was decided that Oren and Jack should take Skid to the animal hospital in Lansing. This would leave Mama and Latonya all night without a man to protect them. While this didn't bother the women that much, it bothered Oren and Jack. Despite Mama's advice not to, Jack insisted on yelling up the stairs at Aunt Grace and telling her to shape up and keep alert. She hollered back down, and told him to keep alert himself. Next Jack called Blue's brother and asked him to look in on Mama and Latonya. Tuffcity was too small and Fritz Bell was too foolish to be any protection, but Jack commanded them both to guard.

While Jack was talking to Mama, and Latonya was fixing a spot in the car for Skid, Oren slipped back into the purple bedroom to have a word with Spiro Spill.

"Listen, Spiro. I see your essence hiding behind the curtain. We all know you to be a meek and harmless ghost, but a ghost is still a ghost and should act like a ghost. Evil people are as frightened as good people when they see a ghost. So if it becomes necessary, you leave your purple room and take care of my mother and my sister. Scare the pants off anybody who comes around. You can do it, Spiro Spill."

The moving car sealed them off together into their own private little world. Skid rested between them, his ears sticking up over the box.

"Jack," Oren fussed, "even though you tranquilized him, Skid's heart is beating fast."

"Fast is normal for a cat's heart," Jack said.

"What about his cancers?" Oren felt Skid's old familiar lumps.

"Tumors grow slowly in old cats. Perhaps we will leave them alone. I will need to take tests and consult with my colleagues on that one."

"Personally, Jack, I don't believe in putting animals out of their misery. Let them stay around and hurt like the rest of us. That's what I always say."

"We will make any decision together, but you have to trust me, Oren."

"Why?"

"Because everything I know about veterinarian medicine, I learned to prepare me for this moment."

That didn't make sense, but Jack meant well. Oren watched the clean snow swirling outside the car window. Now that they were clear of Detroit and its suburbs, he could see lights inside houses and barns. Even in the dark, he could see the open space between the houses. He fell asleep wondering about the mothers, fathers, brothers, and sisters living inside far-apart houses. What did they think about? What did they have to fear? When Oren woke up they still hadn't reached Lansing. Jack had a distance to drive when he courted Mama.

"Oren, are you awake?"

"Yes." Oren put a finger under Skid's chin and started up the old cat's purr.

"Oren, I want to talk to you about something important. I asked your mother to marry me the night Brenda went into the hospital, and then I asked her again tonight."

Jack's timing was off. That was the reason he was at odds with Mama.

"She didn't put me off tonight. She intends talking it over with Latonya and Brenda, but I suspect that I need your permission."

No big surprise. He'd seen it coming. In the pause that followed, Oren admitted to himself that his mother and sisters did depend on him to make the big decisions.

"What do you love about Mama?" Oren opened thoughtfully.

Jack was quick and ready to answer. "Sarah is adorable when she is happy, lovely when she is sad, cute when she is stubborn. I admire neatness. Sarah and Latonya pick up ice-cream wrappers and old beer cans after messy people they don't even know. Your mother is brave and loyal and she has a great sense of humor."

Oren knew that his mama did not have a great sense of humor. She and Jack laughed together over really dumb stuff. "Mama has a much better sense of serious," Oren corrected. So far, he wasn't impressed.

"That too," Jack agreed. "Another virtue I love about your mother, she really listens when I talk. Some of my past dates just pretended to listen when I talked."

Oren let that one go by.

"I most respect and honor the way your mother, with no marketable skills, took over the care and feeding of three children and a middle-aged drunk." Jack politely refrained from mentioning Aunt Grace, who never paid her share, but Oren was still not satisfied.

"And now here is a really big consideration—your mother passed along all of her sweetness and integrity to her children. I would be honored to have you for a son and your sisters for my daughters." Jack rested on that note like he had the deal sewed up.

"I understand where you're coming from, Jack," Oren said. "Here is the big question. What do you have to give back?"

"A marketable skill?" Jack was doubtful.

"Big deal. We've been doing fine without one." Oren waited for Jack to pass a truck before he laid down the important conditions. "What if Granddaddy recovers from his Red Rose disease and wants to come home to us?"

"Then your Granddaddy will be my father," Jack stated firmly.

"What about Aunt Grace, Dink, Dede, and Fritz Bell?"

Jack tried for a compromise on that one. "Your Aunt Grace and her family are moving into Jefferson Project."

Oren stayed solid. He knew Aunt Grace would seek them out for family dinners and loans. Oren also knew that Aunt Grace intended gifting them with Fritz. Jefferson Project and all of Aunt Grace's church friends had rejected Fritz. It was doubtful if the dog pound would take the deadhead dog.

Oren's silence gave Jack the message. "Your Aunt Grace will be my Aunt Grace. If necessary, I will take Fritz Bell or find him a suitable home."

"How about Spiro Spill?"

"Your ghost will be my ghost." Jack shouted this one out because he had never minded Spiro that much.

"If we decide to marry you, where will we live?" Oren was getting to the end of the list. Good thing. The next exit off the freeway was Lansing.

"I'll try to set up a practice in Detroit." The poor guy sounded whipped. He must really love Mama.

"If Mama, Latonya, and Brenda accept you, Jack Daniels, so will I. No need to move your animal practice until you're ready. We can settle in and made do in Lansing for a while, and that includes Skid, Tuffcity, Spiro Spill, and Fritz Bell."

There was something very important they hadn't talked about, but Oren decided to save it. He had never told it to a soul before, but if Jack was going to marry them, he had a right to know. It would have to wait.

Jack introduced Oren around the animal hospital to all of his colleague friends as his son. It seemed to give him a kick to do so. The vets were taking a real interest in Skid. Skid's cage was in the tender-loving-care section, where there were always people working around to talk to him. Oren and Jack said good night to their cat. Skid didn't mind them going.

Jack lived in a fancy apartment called a condominium. First thing, Oren called Mama and Latonya.

"Mama, Skid's operation takes place in the morning. He has no internal injuries. The house only got his tail. He may be in the hospital for a while, but his chances for recovery look good. Jack and I will be back in Detroit in time to take you and Latonya to see Brenda in the hospital late tomorrow afternoon. How was Brenda today?"

"Good, Oren. She is now drawing pictures of a ship called the *Fitzgerald.* Her doctor thinks that might be a good sign."

"Why?"

"There were nowhere near the number of lost souls on the *Fitzgerald* as on the *Titanic.*"

"That is good news, Mama. Mama, I have decided Jack can't keep up making this trip each day. Have a heart. I think that we should all get married to each other, and live in Lansing, at least for a while. What do you think?"

Mama said there were a few things to work out but she would think on it. She put Latonya on the phone, and Latonya agreed with his decision.

"Latonya, try to survive Jefferson School on your own tomorrow. Better days are coming. The hour is too late for me to look around much, but Jack's condo has a great kitchen and there's a swimming pool in the yard. Me and Jack are a little worried as to whether our pets will be accepted in this place, but we'll work it out somehow. That's what families do."

"Oren, what about the treasure? I think it's church honest that we should keep it, but Mama isn't sure."

"You work that one out, Latonya. Any trouble?"

"Like what?"

"Like dangerous visitors."

"Aunt Grace came down to comfort Mama and me and help us straighten up the house, but she left in a hurry. She was trying to take down sinking-ship pictures off the wall in the purple bedroom and throw them out, when she claims a cold, pushy mist tried to get her. The fact is, Aunt Grace is moving her family out tomorrow. Blue's brother says that they are going to take down the house next door tomorrow. It could be partly or mostly gone by the time you get home."

Before he could turn over in his twin bed and go to sleep, Oren was bothered by what was left unsaid.

"Jack?"

"Yes, Oren."

"You ever heard of any men who call themselves Martin Grainer or P. A. Parker?"

There was a quiet pause. Oren thought that Jack had dropped off to sleep.

"I know of a Martin Grainer and a P. A. Parker by reputation," Jack said.

"Who are the ones you know by reputation?"

"Martin Grainer is a state representative. He represents your district in Detroit, but he works here in Lansing. As you know, Oren, Lansing is the capital of Michigan. As for

P. A. Parker, he is a millionaire who owns a string of funeral homes all over the city. He is famous for organizing charity drives. There could be more than two by that name."

"The ones you know of. Are they big shots?"

"The biggest."

"Jack, both Granddaddy and Fred were doing something illegal in the house next door. Their part was bottom level, and they were not supposed to know much, but Fred and Granddaddy were both smart for their age. When they drew ships with Brenda, they didn't give their ships the names of real ships like Brenda did. They called their ships names like *Martin Grainer* and *P. A. Parker.* They gave other names to other pictures that don't sound like ship names. Some of their ships have numbers written on the bow or the sails."

"I hear what you're saying, Oren. Fred and Granddaddy wrote down information that they had picked up in the house. The brains behind organized crime might well come from high office, but Crayola pictures of sinking ships isn't much proof."

"Mama would insist on giving what we knew to the police. It could be very dangerous to be part of a pickie honest family like the Bells." Oren gave it to Jack straight. "Granddaddy's and Fred's ships are taped on the wall of the purple bedroom where Brenda put them. I think I have to tell Mama what I suspect."

"I think you're right,"

"Does it scare you, Jack?"

"It scares me, Oren."

"Another thing, Jack." Oren told the story of the ceremony.

"The ceremony is nothing but a made-up superstition; but Oren, if it gives Latonya some peace of mind, I can see why you went along with it."

"But I accidentally did open my eyes, and terrible things did happen."

"They would have happened anyway, Oren. We both know that."

He didn't know that for sure, but he went on. "Jack, it might be a danger for you to be in our family."

"You promised, Oren Bell. You are not getting out of our deal. I helped you get Brenda off the *Titanic,* didn't I? You have to deal me in."

"You're in. You're in. Now get to sleep. You got an important operation to perform in the morning." That Jack would go through anything to be in their family. "Jack, should I ever tell Latonya that I opened my eyes?"

"I wouldn't."

Jack was right. It was brave and honest to fight organized crime, but foolhardy to take Latonya's ceremony away from her.

Late afternoon. As soon as they drove up in the driveway, Oren saw a big hole and piles of brick where the house next door had once stood. In one day, it had disappeared. He was glad that he hadn't watched its passing. There was a truck parked in the driveway, and Uncle Penn was loading the last of Aunt Grace's belongings inside. Aunt Grace, Dink, and Dede were sitting up front in the truck, dressed up and fit to go. Jack and Oren gave them a nod and hurried inside their house to collect a few hugs for saving Skid.

There was a party going on inside and it didn't stop or even slow down when Oren and Jack made their entrance. They received a few nods, and Mr. Shell said, "How's old Skid doing?" and Mama said, "Pull up a chair." Sitting around the big, round dining room table were Mama, Latonya, Mr. Shell, Ms. Pugh, Wesley, Blue, and Whitey. Buttercup was on the floor sniffing Tuffcity. Most astounding, the two red eyes of the house next door had been removed from their sockets and were propped up carefully against the wall. The party people eating their cookies and ice cream weren't paying the glass windows a whit of attention. Latonya, back in her top form, was playing her pie-in-the-sky game and the company was suffering along in good spirits.

"Tomorrow," Latonya said, "Mama, Mr. Shell, and Ms. Pugh are going to city hall, and our house will be saved. Alleluia and Praise the Lord."

"We actually only have an appointment in the city planning office," Mama said, "but the prospects look very good."

"The prospects look great," Ms. Pugh said. "What we have here is a historic dwelling in excellent condition."

Oren knew how to make counterattacks in Latonya's pie-in-the-sky game. If he moved in quick he might be able to get others on his side.

"Mama is out of work and Aunt Grace has moved on," he said.

As usual, Latonya topped his downer with an upper. "Mr. Shell is going to open a music studio in the top flat and he is more reliable about paying rent than Aunt Grace. Spiro's original music school was located upstairs. Sounds from promising new musicians will gladden the heart and quiet the spirit of Spiro Spill."

"If the city lets me move in, and that's a big *if*," Mr. Shell said.

"The Spiro Spill School for Performing Arts." Ms. Pugh extended Latonya's pie. "That special school for disadvantaged, talented youngsters will be right here."

"And if we can get the land next door, Jack could build an animal hospital for disadvantaged sick and injured city animals." Latonya was on a pie high.

Oren countered. "Jack needs to get paid for his marketable skill because he has a family to support. Mr. Shell needs to get paid for his music teaching, so he can eat and put gas in his old Thunderbird."

"I'll pay for my music lessons," Wesley said.

"You can have my gold record," Blue volunteered.

"Mine too," Whitey said.

"Oren," Mama said, "Latonya and I took those records to the police. We made a claim on them. They might be held for months before our claim is recognized, but I think eventually we'll end up with Spiro's gold." As usual, she was playing on both sides of the game.

"Carl and Jack are not the only ones here with marketable skills," Ms. Pugh said. "The board of education is giving me a respectable raise to tutor homebound sick and handicapped children; and Sarah has an interview next week for the position of research assistant in a prominent downtown Detroit law firm."

It was time to stop playing games. "What are those eyes

doing in our dining room?" Oren screamed. "Why are they staring at us?"

There was a moment of silence. The company regarded the ruby windows. They had been cleaned up to a healthy, handsome glow and appeared almost friendly.

"The workmen left them here for tonight," Mama said. "The city intends to put them up at public auction. I want these windows for our home, wherever that may be." Mama was dead serious.

"Wherever," Jack said.

Oren knew Jack would move mountains to get those windows for Mama. She wanted them more than a diamond ring. Oren might as well give up. The eyes of the house would follow them forever.

There were no more wild pie-in-the-sky schemes, so the party started to wind down. Jack finally got to tell how he had saved the life of Skid the cat, but both Jack and Oren kept still about the ship pictures. Time for that later. Ms. Pugh, Mr. Shell, and Buttercup left together. The families of Wesley, Whitey, and Blue showed up and carried them off, but Latonya was invited to sleep over at Wesley's house the following week. Finally Jack and Mama said it was time for them to go to the hospital and see Brenda. Latonya and Oren were locked in for the evening to take care of themselves.

"Latonya, I was telling Jack about the music we heard Spiro play on the organ. He says some old organs have rolls of music inside that play by themselves."

"Pipe organs don't have rolls of music that play by themselves. Can't you accept a gift from a ghost, Oren?"

"Why do we have to keep those windows?"

"The least we can do is give Spiro's beautiful red eyes a chance to look out from a God-fearing house."

He guessed it was the least they could do. Spiro had lived with them during their growing-up years. Was it possible that it was Spiro and not the ceremony that had been protecting them from the dark side of the city? As Oren looked at the red eyes, an idea gripped him.

"Latonya, I just remembered something that I saw in the attic when I was up getting Brenda off the roof. It didn't mean anything to me then, but it does now. We have to go up in the attic before Mama and Jack get home to tell us we shouldn't. Don't be afraid. I'll take care of you."

"I'm not afraid of a common attic, Oren. If you feel the force of an idea, we had better follow it."

Latonya was keeper of the keys, so there was no problem there. They stomped on each step going upstairs, as if the noise of their feet would drive away any presence in the upstairs flat. The rooms were empty of furniture, the windows exposed. Aunt Grace had been neat in leaving. Nothing remained but the white carpeting. They felt like running through the soft, high shag with their bare feet, but some energy was urging them on to the business at hand. Latonya held the flashlight for Oren. Surefooted, he slipped up through the hole in the ceiling, then reached down to give her a hand. They both knew where they were going. They avoided the sight of the open cavity where Oren had rescued Brenda, and made their way to the opposite farthest, darkest corner under the eaves.

"I remember. We found this box of records when we were kids, but it didn't look interesting to us then," Latonya said.

"It looks interesting to me now," Oren said. "Help me slide it. The bottom might fall out."

The box was heavy enough to suggest he was right about the contents. They dragged it to the hole. Oren went down first and then stood back. Latonya pushed and shoved the box through the hole. A few delicate old records on top sailed free and landed safely on the deep white shaggy rug. The heavy yellow discs on the bottom came down like bricks.

"I guess Spiro didn't believe in putting his gold in banks," Oren said. "Good thing he held back from taking most of it over to the house next door. I wonder if it's real? There's such a thing as fool's gold."

"It's real, Oren. I know it's real."

"If it is real, we probably won't be allowed to keep it."

"Spiro doesn't have any relatives. The gold is inside our house. Brenda says when you find golden treasures from a sinking ship, you get to keep it. We'll see, Oren."

They moved the windows from the dining room to the living room, and then sat together on the living room sofa and studied them. The beautiful glass panes reflecting their image seemed to be lighter color, nearer to peaceful pink.

"Latonya, all the gold in the world won't make all your pie-in-the-sky schemes come true."

"I do know the difference between dream stuff and real stuff, Oren Bell. What you don't realize is, sometimes real stuff is just dream stuff while other times dream stuff is real as rain."

"Sure, Latonya. Some of your dream stuff might come true. One out of ten is a possibility."

"You know, Mama says that Brenda doesn't talk about Spiro anymore. I fear that if Brenda doesn't see and communicate with him, you and I might forget about him. That poor, sad spirit always tried to do his best by us, and that's the most you can expect out of a person or a ghost. Don't you ever forget Spiro Spill, Oren."

"I won't."

"Oren, tomorrow I think we should take Fred and Granddaddy's ship pictures to the police."

Oren stared at her. She knew.

"There's information in those pictures that will help honest, hard working detectives catch Fred's murderers and make our city safe."

"You think there's enough honest people to save the city, Latonya?"

"I do. Whenever evil dishonors a place, there are powers to save."

"We don't have to go through any more ceremonies, do we, Latonya?"

"No more ceremonies. You did it right this year, Oren Bell."

Barbara Hood Burgess and her husband live in
Livonia, Michigan, and have four grown children
and six grandchildren. A self-described late
bloomer, she recently earned a B.A. from Wayne
State University. She has written musical theater
projects and operettas for church, scout, and
children's groups, and has worked at several jobs,
among them teacher's aide and veterinarian's assistant.
"Best of all," she says, "I like telling ghost stories
to young people."

OREN BELL is her first novel.